He hadn't been in touch.

He might be packing u
would surely have hea
Mountain by now. Wha
could make her believe
and a veil and the prom
hadn't been heading ir
nothing to each other about anything like that.

"But we never actually ended it," he repeated now.

"No, we didn't."

"And if you hadn't gotten pregnant, what would have happened? Were you planning to end it, before that happened?"

"Not at that point, I—"

"Not at that point?"

"We met at a bar in a resort town, Mac. In that situation, you're not looking for something long-term, and you kind of assume the other person isn't, either."

"Right." After a moment, he added quietly, "Are you really that cynical and hard-edged? You were that ready to dump the whole thing the moment it threatened to go deeper?"

"No! I was...really enjoying it, if you want the truth. Every bit of it."

Scaring myself a little bit, wondering once or twice if I was being played.

* * *

THE CHERRY SISTERS:
Three sisters return to their childhood home
in the mountains—and find the love of a lifetime!

Dear Reader,

Would you describe yourself as the outdoorsy type? Or are you someone who much prefers to tuck yourself cosily away indoors during the cold of winter?

Like my heroine in this story, I'm a mix of both. As far as I'm concerned, there's nothing like fresh air and beautiful views and a good hike or swim or ski. There's also nothing like that delicious feeling of coming back to a warm house and something good to eat after a bracing few hours in the open.

Lee has her life set up exactly the way she wants in this area. She's a ski instructor in Colorado by day, with a very nice arrangement as live-in caretaker for an eleven-million-dollar mansion that occupies much of her free time but gives her access to an open fire, a Jacuzzi and seven bathrooms.

Yet when the story opens, she's not in Colorado— she's back home in upstate New York, staring down a very angry Mac Wheeler, who has followed her halfway across the country to say his piece. What has happened to throw both of these characters so far beyond their comfort zone?

Well, you've probably guessed the answer to this from the book's title. More important, however, *how* did it happen, and what are they going to do about it?

I hope you enjoy Lee and Mac's tumultuous relationship, and their equally tumultuous journey.

Lilian Darcy

The Baby Made at Christmas

Lilian Darcy

HARLEQUIN® SPECIAL EDITION®

Recycling programs
for this product may
not exist in your area.

ISBN-13: 978-0-373-65779-7

THE BABY MADE AT CHRISTMAS

Copyright © 2013 by Lilian Darcy

All rights reserved. Except for use in any review, the reproduction
or utilization of this work in whole or in part in any form by any
electronic, mechanical or other means, now known or hereafter
invented, including xerography, photocopying and recording, or in
any information storage or retrieval system, is forbidden without
the written permission of the publisher, Harlequin Enterprises Limited,
225 Duncan Mill Road, Don Mills, Ontario M3B 3K9, Canada.

This is a work of fiction. Names, characters, places and incidents are
either the product of the author's imagination or are used fictitiously, and
any resemblance to actual persons, living or dead, business establishments,
events or locales is entirely coincidental.

This edition published by arrangement with Harlequin Books S.A.

For questions and comments about the quality of this book, please contact us
at CustomerService@Harlequin.com.

® and TM are trademarks of Harlequin Enterprises Limited or its corporate
affiliates. Trademarks indicated with ® are registered in the United States Patent
and Trademark Office, the Canadian Trade Marks Office and in other countries.

Printed in U.S.A.

Books by Lilian Darcy

LILIAN DARCY

has written nearly eighty books for Silhouette Romance, Harlequin Special Edition and Harlequin Medical Romance. Happily married with four active children and a very patient cat, she enjoys keeping busy and could probably fill several more lifetimes with the things she likes to do—including cooking, gardening, quilting, drawing and traveling. She currently lives in Australia but travels to the United States as often as possible to visit family. Lilian loves to hear from readers. You can write to her at P.O. Box 532, Jamison P.O., Macquarie ACT 2614, Australia, or email her at lilian@liliandarcy.com.

Chapter One

Upstate New York, March

"I am so angry with you, Lee." Mac stood there at the bottom of the porch steps, against a backdrop of blooming crocuses in bright yellow and purple, while the still-bare trees gleamed with a coating of ice against a perfect late-March blue sky.

His hair was getting a little long, and he must have combed it back with his fingers because it lay in untidy, slightly wavy strands along the top of his head and down the back of his neck. A glint of sunlight caught his cheekbones, and the shadow above them made his dark eyes seem even darker. His shoulders looked strong and square under his shirt, and he stood with his feet planted on the ground as if ready for a fight with a grizzly bear. He was so gorgeous it almost hurt to look at him.

He hadn't told Lee he was coming, and he'd driven here, he hadn't flown. His familiar dark blue pickup was parked right there, still muddy and speckled with splashes of Colorado mountain road salt even after a journey of two thousand miles.

It spooked Lee that he'd driven all this way without a word of warning. Rattled the cage of her catlike independence, and made her very wary about his reasons. There was a statement in what he'd done. He'd ambushed her deliberately, and she didn't know whether to be angry right back, or fall into his arms, or some third alternative that for the moment she couldn't bring to mind.

It was never meant to get serious....

It was ten in the morning and Lee was still wearing her thick, fluffy, blue robe, wrapped in it for comfort as much as for warmth, because she'd felt disgustingly sick to her stomach since first rolling over in the glorious coziness of her bed at seven.

Her hair hung down around her face in a mess, and she could see it in the corner of her vision, like ropes of caramel taffy. Her mouth still tasted too strongly of mint toothpaste, and of the sweet grapes she'd eaten to mask the mint. When she'd come down to answer the knocking at the office door, she'd expected a delivery of clean linen or liquor supplies or bulk groceries, all of which were due sometime over the next couple of weeks.

Spruce Bay Resort was currently closed, in preparation for the coming spring and summer seasons. It was Monday, but the landscaping crew wasn't here today, thank goodness. Mom and Dad were on the way back to their new home in South Carolina, her sister Daisy and new husband, Tucker, had left for their honeymoon after Saturday's small wedding, and her other sister, Mary Jane, the eldest, had gone away yesterday afternoon for three days of indulgence at a spa in Vermont.

"You'd better come inside," Lee said. Mac was wearing jeans and a blue shirt with the sleeves rolled, comfortable for driving, but not warm enough in the open air chill.

"So angry!" he repeated. "Do you not understand that?"

She forced herself to speak calmly, trying to hose down the mood as best she could. "Well, yes, I do, but we did talk about it. It's not as if I hid anything, or lied to you."

"You talked. I was too stunned to react. I had things to think about, too, remember? And by the time I reacted, you'd just…gone."

Because we never once said it was serious, so why should that change now?

"Want some coffee?" she asked.

"*That's* what you have to offer?"

"It's a start, isn't it?" It had been a start for them, before. "We obviously need to talk. About why you're here. And how long you're staying. And it's cold. So you should come inside, and we should have coffee. We both like coffee."

"You drive me crazy."

"I know."

"You are *nothing* like my sister."

"I know that, too."

"Or my mother."

"So you tell me."

"Or any woman I've ever known." She was like a cat, he'd told her the day after they'd met, and since then she'd embraced the idea. She was good with being a cat. The independence, the pleasing herself, the appreciation for comfort and warmth, but quite a taste for curiosity and adventure, as well.

"Isn't that what you like about me?" She ventured a grin, but he wasn't to be softened so easily.

Because it is *serious.*

"I don't know if I like anything about you right now, Lee Cherry," Mac said. He stepped onto the porch, crossed it in two strides, pushed past her as she pressed her back against the open door. Then he turned around. "What is this? The office? Why are we in here?"

"Yes, it's the office. But there are stairs in back, up to the apartment."

"You're living above the resort office? On your own?" He was looming over her, seeming like too much big, strong, healthy beautiful man for the rather dark and confined space.

He was glaring at her with those dark eyes of his, but then they flicked down. To her lips. Which were suddenly hot and dry. The impenetrable gaze flicked back up before she could even swallow. It almost felt as if he'd kissed her, even though his mouth hadn't come anywhere near hers. She loved the way he kissed.

"With my sister, Mary Jane, at the moment," she answered him, incredibly annoyed to discover that her voice wasn't quite steady. "Except that she's away."

They *had* talked. She hadn't just run out on him. She'd presented him with the whole situation, her decisions and her plan, assuming he'd feel the same way she did, and he had.

He had! He hadn't given her any kind of argument, hadn't said a word about wanting to stay together.

"It's bigger than it looks," she went on, knowing she was giving unnecessary detail about the Cherry family apartment. "It's a real home, Mac, not just 'living above the office.'" She wanted to fill the space with talk, instead of this hyperawareness of his body…of his whole presence. His anger. His attitude. The creeping possibility that she might be in the wrong. "Four bedrooms, kitchen, living room, two bathrooms, above this lower level, which has the office and three storerooms and the double garage. We all lived here, growing up."

"That's your parents and your two sisters, running the resort. And you're the eldest?"

"Middle."

See? How could it have been serious, if you don't even know where I fit in my family?

He ignored her correction. "So coffee is upstairs?"

"Yes." She turned and led the way, relieved that he was the one focusing on mundane detail now.

He followed her. If he'd brought any bags, he'd left them in the pickup. He had his hands free as he came up the stairs behind her, and she remembered all the times he'd followed her up flights of stairs in Colorado and cupped a hand on her butt or wrapped his arms around her and stopped them both in their tracks.

Turned her around.

Kissed her.

More.

It was good to see him. It made her feel like crying, and she didn't want that, not at all. She'd steeled herself to never see him again, to cut off clean from the very nice fling thing they'd had, because wasn't it better that way? She didn't want something that turned messy or ugly or complicated. She didn't want something that dragged itself out for all the wrong reasons.

Better the clean break.

But now he was here, and her body said she was happy about it, despite everything.

They weren't talking. Upstairs, he followed her into the kitchen and she did a wobbly job of getting out coffee and milk and operating the state-of-the-art espresso machine she'd brought with her from Colorado, all of it in a silence he didn't attempt to break. She was aware of his presence with every fiber of her being. The machine began to bubble and hiss, the only thing in the room making any noise.

She turned away from it and there he was, and if the office had seemed too small for his powerful form, the kitchen was even worse. He leaned his hard, jeans-clad butt against the edge of the sink and folded his muscled arms like a nightclub bouncer, and in Colorado she would have gone right up to him and hung off him until he kissed her.

Which would have taken about half a second, and would have been great.

And then one thing would have led to another, because that was what their entire relationship had been about.

Don't you remember that, Mac?

If he didn't, she could remind him.

She should remind him.

Because the fact that their relationship had mainly been based on sex was *important*.

She'd closed the space between them before the plan was even a plan. It really wasn't conscious or deliberate, it just happened, habit more than anything—the habit of wanting him, and of glorying in the delicious confidence that he wanted her and that they fit together in all the best ways. She slid her fingers past those folded arms, slid and sneaked and burrowed until the arms loosened and dropped, letting her reach all the way around his back.

She didn't go for his mouth, just stood there with her hips pressed against his hardening groin, and looked up at him, looked into the gorgeous, familiar pools of dark that were his eyes. It was quite simple, the way it had always been. They wanted each other and enjoyed each other, and there was nothing wrong with that. There was this electric *thing*…feeling, need, recognition… between their two bodies.

They just connected.

They just liked it.

He swore, or groaned, or something. He was still angry, despite the stirring she could feel in his body. She could see it in his eyes and the set of his mouth. He pulled her closer, so that her breasts grazed against him, then pressed hard. She was wearing only the robe, and it was working loose, the tie at the waist slipping its granny knot and the gap between the fluffy blue lapels widening more and more.

He looked down and saw her cleavage, apparently as if it was something new. The sight seemed to make him pause, and she looked down, too. Yes, okay, they were bigger, and they'd been a pretty decent size to begin with. He liked them. He'd lavished them with endless attention in the past.

She looked up into his face and reached to cup his jaw lightly with her hand. This was one of the things *she* liked, knowing how much he wanted her, and playing to it, making him wait or jumping right in, varying their mood together, teasing him terribly, sometimes, and loving it when he teased her back just as much.

She stretched up and planted a soft, questing kiss on that angry mouth. It didn't soften. She kept going, pressing against his stubborn lips, darting out her tongue, deliberately softening and opening, tilting her head, touching his jaw with feathery fingertips.

Still that mouth didn't soften, but at least it kissed back. Oh, boy, did it kiss back! A rough, angry sort of kiss that came with hard arms around her and muscles tense with frustration and need. She guessed a kiss like this was trying to tell her something, but she didn't buy it…even though she liked it, a lot.

You want a kiss, Lee, you'll get a kiss, he seemed to be saying. *You'll get my hands on your butt and my tongue in your mouth and the taste and smell of me, and, yes, it's damned good and we both know it.*

He hadn't shaved since he left Colorado, it felt like. The three-day growth of beard rasped at her skin as his mouth moved against hers, and of course it felt good. It felt fantastic. He smelled good, too—a mix of car freshener and salted nuts and snow. She put her whole heart into kissing him, threading her fingers through his hair, tilted her face to one side, letting her tongue sweep his mouth deeper and deeper, tangling with his. Any minute now, she'd start undressing him, and he'd get rid of her robe in about four seconds—it was already wide-open, and the belt was on the floor—and this would end the way it always did.

But no.

He kept on punishing her with his body, and she couldn't get her hands down to start unfastening his shirt. Still, that didn't matter for now. He pulled her naked hips against the soft rasp of his jeans and tightened his arm muscles until their strength almost hurt, and as far as she was concerned, all he was doing was proving *her* point, not his.

Admit it, Mac….

Admit what?

"No, Lee, hell!" he growled suddenly. "I won't do this." He removed the rough mouth with a last rasp of unshaved jaw across her cheek, grabbed her wrist and pulled her hand away from its sneaky caress of his face, then bracketed her hips and pushed.

He took the two front sections of her robe and lapped

them across each other, his knuckles bumping her breasts. For a fraction of a second she thought he was going to let those knuckles soften and slow, brush them over her darkened nipples, push the robe open again and cup her, but no. Maybe that was just her hungry imagination, or maybe he'd simply taken hold of his willpower and changed his mind.

He bent and picked up the belt of the robe, passed it behind her, then knotted it in front, tight. "We've never had angry sex before, and now's not the time to start."

She stepped back. "Doesn't have to be angry." He looked so good, her heart was pounding, confusing her.

How happy am I that he's here? Too happy. Scary happy. Don't like it.

"Does when I am," he said.

"So what's going to get you to stop being angry?" She took a breath. "And what's going to get you to leave?"

So I feel safe again. Safe from my heart.

The breath went out of him at this, a big whoosh of it, as if she'd punched him in the gut. He pivoted away from her and leaned on the bench. He looked very, very tired, suddenly, and she wondered how long the two thousand miles of driving had taken him. Nonstop it would have to be at least thirty hours. More. Two days, or three? Had he driven at night, or stopped at a motel?

"You want me to leave?" he growled.

She lifted her chin. "If you're angry, yes. If we can't talk, because all that happens is accusations flying back and forth, then yes, it's best if you leave. Don't you think?"

"I'm not leaving."

"So you want us to talk things through?"

"What I want—" He stopped.

She waited.

"I've had some time to think, now. You didn't give me that before."

"You never asked for it, or showed the slightest indication that you needed it."

"Because I was in shock. I was… This is huge, all of it. You don't know—you can't know… You were four or five days ahead of me with what was happening, and it was completely unfair of you to expect me to catch up right away. Maybe I didn't say the right things, but I don't think you did, either." His eyes blazed darkly.

"I tried."

"So did I."

They glared at each other and he pulled at the collar of his shirt as if it was uncomfortable. His hair feathered against the blue fabric, and before she'd even thought about what she was doing, she reached up and tidied it for him so that it sat in neat waves, overlapping his collar by a good two inches. She loved his hair. She loved that he'd forgotten to fight her off, when really she had no right to touch him like this.

"So tell me about your thinking," she said.

He took a big breath. "I want us to try and make a go of this, Lee."

She didn't even know what that meant. Make a go of what? Having sex? Hadn't they done that already? Wasn't that the whole problem?

They'd been far too stunningly successful at the whole point of having sex, and now her idea about what to do next didn't remotely mesh with his. "What do you mean?" she said eventually. Pathetically.

"I'm moving east. Correction, I have moved."

"You've—"

"Brought everything. Wasn't much I really needed. I'll unpack after we've had that coffee."

"Unpack?"

He turned to her again. His mood had—how could you describe it?—changed color, or something. The black obsidian of anger held a gleam of wicked white light. He almost smiled, but not quite. "Didn't you say this place had four bedrooms?"

Chapter Two

Three months earlier, Colorado

Maybe I should have gone home for Christmas.

The Narman family was in residence at their luxurious Aspen vacation home, which meant that caretaker Lee didn't have the run of the house as she always did when they weren't here. They were generous with this. "Of course you must use the whole place. That's exactly what we want. For it to look lived in."

She tried to be generous in return, going above and beyond what they expected of her, airing the huge rooms out whenever she could, and keeping everything scrupulously clean, preparing the house with fresh flowers and freshly made beds and handpicked groceries when they were due to arrive.

It was a cushy arrangement that she had at this place, with its ski-in ski-out access to the Aspen Highlands slopes, and she didn't want it to change. The family usually stayed here only a few weeks a year.

This time, they were spending the full ten days from before Christmas until after New Year's, and they'd brought a large party of family and guests, so that even in the cozy little janitor's apartment on the lowest level of the house, which Lee retreated to when the family was around, she could hear the noise of partying and children, and the frequent heavy clump of boots in the ski room overhead.

She tried to ignore it. It was only six in the evening, so things probably weren't going to quieten down anytime soon. The floorboards were thumping, there was yelling and laughter and music, doors banging, kids crying, the occasional shriek, the sound of water whooshing through the pipes that ran through the ceiling above her head.

Forget her book; she couldn't concentrate on the story. Try some TV. She switched it on, but couldn't find anything that really appealed. How about something to eat? She had deli pasta and sauce in the refrigerator, and had been thinking about a long soak in the tub, followed by the meal, a glass of wine, read her book while she ate…. So cozy and quiet.

"It's not going to work," she said out loud. Living on your own, you did tend to talk to yourself, sometimes. Nothing wrong with that.

But maybe there was something a little wrong with how disappointed she was about the disruption to her quiet, cozy evening.

Maybe I should have gone home, she thought again.

It was just under four weeks since Tucker had called. Tucker, her ex-fiancé, who was now engaged to her baby sister. He'd more or less asked Lee's permission to be in love with Daisy, and while Lee appreciated the gesture and had not the remotest desire to still be engaged to Tucker herself, let alone married to him—it was more than ten years since they'd called it off, after all—there was a tiny part of her that felt…odd about it. Daisy and Tucker were getting married in March.

A seriously tiny part, just to be clear.

Most of the time, Lee felt completely happy about the

whole thing. And if she tried to project what would have happened if she and Tucker had gone through with the wedding…couple of school-age kids by now, not seeing each other that much because the demands of Tucker's landscaping business wouldn't have meshed very well with her own career in mountain sports…

Well, she couldn't picture it at all.

It scared her that she'd come so close to making such a huge mistake.

In other words, yes, she was really happy for them.

All the same, it had seemed like a good idea *not* to go east for Christmas this year. She would go for the wedding. *Must get that organized soon….*

So it was Christmas Eve, and she was on her own. Yes, she had her little tree in the window, with several prettily wrapped gifts beneath. Yes, she was eating baked ham with friends on Christmas night. But still…

She was thirty-three years old. She lived alone and liked it maybe *too* much. Was it just possible she was getting into a rut?

"Okay, you win," she said to the Narman hordes overhead. "I'm going out."

She substituted a quick shower for the long tub soak, dived into a pair of slinky black pants and a sparkly Christmas top she'd planned for tomorrow night, sketched on a little makeup, put in some bright, dangly Christmas-themed earrings, grabbed a big black winter coat and her heeled black faux-fur boots, and went out into the snow to make the easy half mile walk to her favorite Aspen hangout, the Waterstreet Bar.

Nobody was there.

Well, it was crowded, but they were tourists, not locals. No ski instructors, no mountain management people or hospitality staff, none of the year-rounders she saw all the time during the quieter summer months. Where was everyone?

The thought itched in the back of her head that if the Narmans hadn't been having a noisy party tonight, she would have sat all cozy at home the whole evening and never realized that her Christmas Eve was too solitary, that everyone else, friends and casual acquaintances, had other plans tonight.

She went up to the bar and ordered a light beer and a bowl of spicy wings with sour cream, and when the guy behind the bar offered her one of those buzzer thingies that started hopping around on the table and flashing red lights when your order was ready, she shook her head and said, "Nah, I'll wait for it here, thanks."

He looked vaguely familiar, one of the seasonal staff who she'd maybe seen on the slopes, maybe even taught to ski. If they got chatting, she could just stay and eat her wings and drink her beer right here at the bar.

But he was too busy, she soon saw, and he was only about twenty-two. For chatting purposes, he was all about the nineteen-year-old snow bunnies or rich women looking for a short-term good time, with no interest in a hardworking local woman in her thirties who was more athletic than feminine, more striking than pretty.

For the first time in a long while, Lee was suddenly conscious of the nearly eleven-year-old burn scarring on her neck and jaw. She didn't often wear neck-baring clothes, but the Christmas top had been pretty and silly, and she hadn't been able to resist.

The friends she was going to join for dinner tomorrow had seen her scars before, so that was no big deal. They were faded now. Her skin was pale and sort of melty-looking from just above her left jawline to just below her collarbone and out to her shoulder. She'd gotten splashed with hot oil in the kitchen of the restaurant at Spruce Bay when she was around the same age as this barman here, and had spent some time in hospital, dealing with pain and infection and skin grafts.

Old news.

Irrelevant, for a woman who spent most of her time in ski jackets or collared hiking shirts.

It unsettled her to be thinking about it as if it mattered, because it didn't. It really *didn't*. She liked this top. It was fun. If anyone noticed the scarring, and disapproved of her showing it, that was their problem, not hers.

She sat up straighter and wiggled her head a little so that she could feel the tickle of the spangly red-gold-and-green Christmas trees dangling from her ears. The youthful barman delivered her beer and she drawled, "Thanks," and dismissed him from her mind.

"Nice earrings," someone said, close by.

She turned to find an unfamiliar male in a black T-shirt seated on the bar stool beside her. "Oh. Thanks."

He was grinning at her. "If you're wondering how much they caught the light just now, the answer is a lot. I still have spots before my eyes."

"You got me," she said, grinning back. "I did it on purpose. Love dazzling people till they can't see."

"No point in wearing Christmas trees if nobody notices, right?"

"Right."

The twenty-two-year-old thumped two bowls of wings down on the bar, one in front of Lee and one in front of the earring admirer, then reached back to the serving window again and brought out two matching bowls of sour cream. "Snap," said the stranger.

"It's an astonishing coincidence," she agreed in a drawl, since the bar menu at this place had only about three items on it. If you wanted anything more sophisticated than wings, nachos or fries, you had to go through into the section where the tables and booths had actual placemats.

"Not everyone goes for the sour cream," he pointed out. "Right there, that cuts our odds of a match down to about six to one. And when you add in the beer…"

She hadn't noticed the beer until now, but, yes, she discovered, they were drinking the same brand, a local Colorado microbrew. That was the biggest coincidence yet, given that Waterstreet proudly offered something like fifty-six different kinds.

And speaking of coincidences, *he* might not be familiar, but his red ski jacket was. It hung over the low back of the bar stool, exactly the same as the one she had at home, with its resort and designer logos. "You work here," she said, feeling a ridiculous wash of relief that at last here was a comrade-at-arms, a fellow instructor, roughly her own age.

"Since three days ago, yes." He had the jacket, but at some point he'd changed from ski pants and boots into jeans and running shoes, new looking and chunky.

"Me, too," she told him. "Ski school. But seven years, not three days."

"So I've come to the right bar."

It was a statement, not a question, and she didn't quite follow the logic. "Depends what bar you were looking for."

"I meant, if you've lived here seven years and you've chosen this bar, it can't be a pure tourist trap."

"Oh, right, sorry, yeah. Waterstreet isn't upmarket enough for a lot of visitors."

"I like it. Nice crowd."

But he wasn't looking at the crowd. He was look-ing at her.

Something kicked between them. Something Lee hadn't felt in a long time but recognized anyhow. It shocked her that it was this fast and strong and instinc-tive, and her first reaction was to seek a way to pull back, mentally skidding on her heels in panic and get-ting nowhere, like a character in a cartoon.

She asked carefully, "You're new and no one is show-ing you around?" Because he was clearly here on his own.

"I had a late finish today. Someone in the group had a fall and lost confidence at the top of the mountain, and it took me forty-five minutes to get her down. Someone else…Everard—"

"He's a nice guy," she interjected. She worked with him on junior squad coaching.

"He is. He took the rest of my class back down the mountain for me, but by the time I arrived, everyone but him had gone for the day. He's married, wanted to get home. My nervous lady wanted to take me for a drink—we both needed it—but her choice of bar wasn't mine. After she, uh, left, I came looking for somewhere I liked better."

"And you found it."

"And I found it."

The thing kicked again, and robbed Lee of speech. Imagination? She didn't think so. He didn't seem in a hurry to fill the sudden silence. Well, it was filled al-ready, just not with words. He took a pull on his beer and looked at her over the top of the foam, his eyes very dark in contrast to the frothy white.

Am I really going to do this?

It was too fast. She never did anything like this. She hadn't dated anyone in three years, and that had lasted only a couple of months. Before that... What, another two years? Was it really possible she'd had only two boyfriends in five years? Two pretty lame, tame boyfriends, and lame, tame relationships that hadn't ever looked to be going anywhere, and hadn't been all that successful even as short-term flings.

This one, though...

Really? You're deciding this soon?

For a start, she knew nothing about him.

Or else she knew too much. She could list his likely qualities, just by knowing what he did for a living, and that he was new in town, and that he was on his own in a bar at seven in the evening on Christmas Eve. Was a fling with a bachelor ski instructor really what she wanted?

Why not?

"She, uh, left?" Lee mimicked part of his last statement.

He shrugged and gave an apologetic kind of smile. "She was interested in a longer evening. I wasn't."

"Are you usually?"

He said very firmly, "She was nice. Pretty. But no, not with clients."

A handful of words, and they'd covered an awful lot of ground. Lee had learned that he could have slept with an attractive and willing woman tonight, and that he'd turned her down because on principle he didn't get involved with clients.

If he did make a habit of such a thing, she decided, he could probably have had a different bed partner every night. He was pretty good-looking. Yet it seemed he wasn't just about getting women into bed, and was polite enough to go for a drink when a client needed or wanted it, despite his lack of secondary motivation. He'd apparently charmed the pants off this particular one, since she hadn't been ready to let the evening go.

"You?" he added. His voice had dropped in both pitch and volume, and it drew her in, tightened the circle of deepening intimacy around them.

She shook her head. She didn't date clients, either. That kind of thing could get so messy. And she'd never dated another instructor. That particular form of mess might be even worse.

So why am I thinking about it? I don't even know his name.

"It's Mac, by the way," he said, having apparently read her mind. "Mac Wheeler."

"Lee Cherry."

"I've seen your name on the notice board in the ski school office. We must have been at the morning meetings together, the past couple of days, but I don't remember seeing you."

"It's a big ski school."

"I'm still finding my feet. New town. Back instructing. I haven't done it for a while."

"Oh, you haven't?"

"I'd moved over into the administration side, at a resort that will remain nameless for the moment."

"Ah."

She wasn't exactly asking for an explanation, but he gave her one anyhow. "Didn't see eye to eye with the boss on a certain personal issue. Flung down the gauntlet at the wrong moment. Not that I regret it. It was the only choice."

"Flung down the gauntlet? This is the way you talk?" *When you talk, which at first we weren't, and which I*

*have a feeling we might not be doing for all that much
longer...*

"I've been reading a *really* long fantasy series. The
vocabulary is starting to stick. I quit, if you prefer it
simple, and there was nothing more for me in Sn— I'll
tell you where when we know each other better."

"Right, *when*," she replied mildly, in a drawl, because she didn't want his assumptions to get too out
of hand.

Even though his assumptions are correct...

He gave a slow smile, and said in a tone of meek
apology, "If?" There was nothing remotely meek or
apologetic about him.

They lasted three hours in the bar, which was pretty
impressive, she considered. It was clear where this was
going to end, but they weren't in a hurry to get there.
They shared another bowl of wings, with fries, and each
had another beer before they both switched to soda. He
called it pop, which told both of them that they weren't
from the same part of the country.

He was from Idaho, it turned out. "Coeur d'Alene.
My mom's a teacher, my dad works for the city. I have
a sister there, too, married with two kids."

Lee supplied her own basic biography. Mom, Dad
and two sisters. Opposite side of the country, but strong
similarities all the same. Both of them were mountain-
born, growing up in resort towns where dramatic vistas of lakes and mountains were a major part of the
attraction. Both of them had started skiing as kids and
then turned to it as a career, although Mac had fairly
quickly moved into the management side, and had a
degree in the field.

"Can I ask about your skin?" he said at one point.
"Do you mind?"

"Of course I don't mind. It was a kitchen accident," she answered. "Big splash of hot oil. Eleven years ago, nearly."

"Right." He nodded. "I thought it looked like a burn. Must have hurt."

"They gave me nice drugs."

He laughed, and they were done talking about her scars, so check off another item on the biography list.

But who was she kidding? Maybe they covered those kinds of things, but it was all the stuff going on underneath the conversation that really counted. The way his shoulder brushed against her when he reached for his drink, and the way she leaned into the contact instead of away from it. The smiles, lazy and slow, making her feel like the cat that got the cream.

The noise of the bar faded into the background. In fact, the noisier it became, the more they seemed enclosed in their own little cocoon, having to lean even closer to hear each other speak. They were comfortable with one another, instantly familiar.

He was the one to say it, finally, muttering just inches from her mouth, "So shall we get out of here?"

"Let's."

"Where?" he asked, as they threaded their way between the crowded tables. He was behind her, not touching her to claim possession the way some men did. She liked that he could keep his hands to himself, in his jacket pockets, and didn't feel the need to signal the kind of look-what-I've-got message that she'd seen played out in this very bar by countless couples.

Once in the snowy dark, she suggested, "My place?" and he nodded.

"Has to be better than mine. Haven't had a chance

to find anything decent, yet. I'm sleeping on a friend's couch."

"Boy, you really did come here in a hurry."

He shook his head, looking angry. "I don't handle unjustified accusations well."

"No?"

"Boss thought I was coming on to his wife. I wasn't."

"Did *she* think you were?"

"No. And she told him he was wrong, but that was *after* he'd tried to punch me, so as far as I was concerned, it was too late. He drinks too much. He's a disaster. He wasn't going to let it go. He would have been watching me every moment from then on. He was on a hair trigger about it." Mac shook his head again. "Better for all three of us if I took myself out of the equation."

"But it's mucked up your life, somewhat."

"My life will get back on track." He sounded very confident, and she believed him. He was the kind of man who exuded a quiet certainty about his own identity and strength.

Maybe that's why...

Why she was inviting a near-stranger back to her apartment. Why she had no doubts about it at all. Why she wanted him in the first place.

They walked, the soles of their boots crunching on ice and gritty road. He took note of the direction they were going, and said, "You must be in a pretty nice part of town."

And just at that moment they came around a bend and there was the Narmans' place, all lit up, looking like the eleven-million-dollar property that it was. He stopped short. "This?"

"Yes, but—"

He was looking at her, appalled, as if she'd grown three heads. "I thought you were an instructor."

"I am. I live here, but it's not mine. Lordy, no! I wouldn't even *want* a place like this. I'm the janitor, part-time."

"The janitor."

"Caretaker. House sitter. Housekeeper. Person who calls repairmen. Jill-of-all-trades. I have a tiny apartment under the floor, where I am intimately acquainted with the flow of water in the pipes, as you soon will be, also." She gave him a jaunty grin, because, really, the pipes weren't that bad.

He burst out laughing. "You are my kind of woman, Lee."

Chapter Three

Upstairs, the Narmans' party was still in full swing.

Lee and Mac crept around the side of the house to her little side entrance, where the snow she'd had to dig out from the steps three days ago made gleaming blue-white walls on either side. Nobody saw them. All the drapes were open, but nobody was looking out into the dark. They were all too busy spilling drinks on the floor and filling the trash cans with empty bottles.

"Will you have to clear up after that lot?" Mac asked as he waited for her to get out her key.

"Not personally, but I'll have to organize the cleaners first thing in the morning. This is not a planned event, unfortunately."

"Will you be able to get anyone? It'll be Christmas Day."

"I have some good arrangements in place with local companies. Cleaners, caterers, repairmen, suppliers. They know the drill, and the Narmans pay well. I told them the family was bringing in a big group and they might be needed at short notice. It only happens a couple of times a year." She turned the key in the lock and he followed her in, and reality hit.

She was here, in her own private space, with a man she hadn't even known when she'd left her cozy nest four hours ago. She had a moment of utter panic, and didn't know where to begin. Offer him—? Tell him—? Touch him and—?

She turned, on the point of giving a babbled apology. *You'll have to go. I don't do this. I really don't.*

But then she saw him standing there, hands deep in the pockets of that familiar red ski jacket, and she felt a rush of calm—if calm could come in a rush. He wasn't lunging for her. He wasn't leering with intent. He was simply taking a quiet look around. At her bookshelves. At her neat kitchen, where the expensive espresso coffee machine was her only visible indulgence.

"I can see why you live here on your own," he said. "There's not a whole lot of room for two."

"It suits me. I'm on the slopes all day. Nice to have a warm rabbit burrow to come home to."

"I guess. You don't get lonely?"

"No, I like it. You?"

"Mostly in the past I've shared with a couple of guys. Ones who aren't total pigs, but who also don't have to vacuum the windowsills twice a day. Don't know what I'll do for accommodation here."

"Those guys exist? Really?"

He laughed, then looked at her open bedroom door, through which he could see the double bed, covered in its indulgent piles of bright silk pillows and thick, puffy comforter. She hated sleeping in a warm room, and always turned the heating way down at night, but loved to snuggle under cozy covers.

Maybe not tonight. Tonight the comforter might have to go, and they would need the air warm....

He stopped looking at her apartment and looked at her instead. "Nice coffee machine."

"Makes nice coffee."

"Want to make some now?" he suggested.

"Sure. Want to help?"

She liked that he was as nervous as she was, that he wanted to ease into this, take some time. When she went into the kitchen, he came after her. "So what's my job?"

"Choosing mugs. Top shelf, there. Or on the hooks."

"You don't trust me with the technical part?"

"It's a one-person job." Which she did with her back to him, while she heard him clinking the mugs.

"You have too many mugs for a kitchen this size, I would have thought," he said.

"I like nice ones." Pretty mugs, cute mugs, silly mugs, clever mugs. She knew she had too many. At least sixty, which was why she needed a whole shelf, and half a wall covered in hooks. Turning, she found he'd chosen two from a set she especially loved.

"These are great," he said. "Book covers."

"Penguin Classics paperbacks, the original cover designs. Don't you love buying on the internet?"

"Why these?" In his hand, he rotated the purple-and-white of Virginia Woolf's *A Room of One's Own.* On the counter sat a green-and-white Agatha Christie, *The Body in the Library.*

"I have others. *Pride and Prejudice. Great Expectations.* And there are heaps in the series that I don't have."

"So you don't need to read the books, you just buy the mugs."

"No, I've read the books. I only bought the ones I'd read."

"Is that a rule? You can't drink from the mug unless you've read the book."

She grinned. "Yep." It wasn't really a rule, as such, but it was a nice idea. "I'm very, very strict with my guests on that."

"I'd better pick a different mug, then," he said. "Hope I'm not out of luck. Really don't want to have to drink from…" He examined a few more, ones that didn't have book covers on them. "…a basket of kittens, or something with a china frog inside it, while you're being all intellectual with Virginia Woolf. Aha, okay, good." He'd found George Orwell's *1984,* in orange and white.

It ended the conversation, and the coffee wasn't quite ready yet. Upstairs, somebody changed the music and the thumping acquired a different rhythm, just as loud, possibly Coldplay. Lee and Mac faced each other, waiting. He stepped closer. Very close. Well, it was a tiny kitchen. He reached out and touched the scarring on her shoulder. "We didn't quite finish about your skin. Does it bother you if it's touched?"

"Not anymore. It used to."

He nodded, hand still resting lightly there. She waited for more, but apparently there wasn't any. She liked that he'd said something, rather than pretending there weren't any issues. And she liked that he'd kept it short and practical, both here and back at the bar, with no meaningless gushes of sympathy.

"This is good," he said. "Don't you think?"

He didn't spell out what *this* was, but she thought she knew. The way they were talking, the ease in being close to each other. The way they could both handle the occasional silence. The fact that he'd found a mug he was permitted to drink from because he'd read the book—even though they'd both made up that rule on the spot.

"Mmm, it is," she answered.

Something vibrated in the air between them and she stepped into it. They were so close now that their thighs were touching, and if she hadn't arched her back a little, she would have been leaning against his chest.

She *wanted* to lean against his chest, but for people who'd only met four hours ago, they were taking this pretty slow. She didn't want to rush a kiss or a close embrace. He touched her mouth with the pad of his thumb, then bent lower and tasted her, just the tiniest brush of a kiss on her mouth. "Nice," he said softly. "We're going to make this so nice."

She liked that he'd chosen such a plain, simple word. He wasn't promising to rock her world, baby. As a thank-you for his down-to-earth ego, she kissed him back. Longer this time. Sweeter. Then she broke away, just as he had done, so that they could assess what had happened up to this point.

He grinned, and it looked like relief, and she felt it, too.

Whew! So far, not a disaster. Let's cautiously keep going and see if we can make it stay that way. Or even get better.

"Coffee's ready," she said.

"Better pour it, then." He slid Virginia Woolf and George Orwell closer. Lee preheated the cups with hot water, steamed the milk, started the flow of rich, dark liquid through the spigot and into each mug.

And then they didn't sit down. They just stood there in the kitchen, drinking the coffee with their backsides pressed against the edge of the counter and an arm around each other. "It's really good coffee," he said.

"I know. I have to ration myself. This'll keep me awake half the night, drinking it so late."

"Which is good, in my opinion. Kind of like the idea of you awake."

"It does tend to enhance the experience."

A little later, when the coffee was nearly gone, he told her, "You have foam on your top lip."

"Oh." She reached up and brushed it off.

"You know you weren't supposed to do that, right? I was supposed to kiss it off."

"In fact, I didn't really have foam there at all."

"No, you did. But you took care of it. Sadly."

"You don't need an excuse to kiss me, do you?"

"Valid point." He put down his empty mug, took hers and put that down, also, peeled himself away from the edge of the counter and folded her in his arms.

They must have kissed for…oh, hours. They kissed until she was boneless, until her vision blurred, until she was practically a puddle on the floor, soft all over, throbbing.

She'd never known such kissing. So warm and strong and lazy. So hot and deep and luscious and perfect. So much an experience with her whole body. He made it totally clear that he was in no rush, and neither was she. Maybe no one had invented anything beyond kissing. Maybe kissing was the whole point, the be-all and end-all, the pinnacle.

Or maybe it wasn't.

Finally, he took his mouth away long enough to say lazily, "Think they've quietened down, upstairs."

She listened, beyond the slow thump of her heart and the giddiness in her brain. The music was turned off. There was no more laughing and yelling. She could hear a couple sets of footsteps going back and forth, and the occasional sound of a low-pitched voice. "I thought they might go on later than this. What's the time?" She heard the creakiness in her own voice.

Mac peered over her shoulder at the microwave clock. "Midnight. Well, twenty after." He sounded creaky, too. Rusty, as if too much kissing had clamped up their vocal cords.

She groped for rational thought. "I guess it's Christmas tomorrow. There are some kids visiting who are still Santa age. Parents probably wanted to get the gifts under the tree, before they're awakened at the crack of dawn. I noticed they'd corralled off the room with the big tree, and weren't using it for the party. They're saving that for their gift opening, tomorrow."

"It's Christmas today," he corrected.

"After midnight. You're right."

"So...Merry Everything!" He smiled at her.

"Merry what?"

"Christmas itself is not the top thing in my mind, right now. So I'm leaving it open. Hoping there's some merry other stuff about to happen pretty soon."

"Well, Merry Everything back at you, then."

"Pretty merry so far." He pressed his cheek against hers, then turned his head a little so that he was kissing her again. "You have the best mouth...." he whispered. "The best body."

"You're not bad, either," she whispered back.

"So that's how we're going to play it? I tell you you're the best, and you tell me I'm not bad?"

"It's not a competition," she said lightly.

"And yet I really like to win." His breath heated her ear.

"So do I."

"I'm taking your top off...."

"Not if I take it off first."

"You do like to win. But you won't win this." He peeled the red-and-green Christmas garment upward in one swift movement, taking her by surprise. When he ran his hands deliberately over the generous curves of her already acutely sensitized breasts on the way, she gasped and forgot about fighting back. How could anything feel this good?

He reached around to the back of her bra and turned his slight clumsiness with the hooks into a caress, thumbing the knobs of her spine with silky touches. The hooks stayed stubborn. "I *am* going to win the bra!" Lee said, because she knew the quirks of this one and had beaten them before.

Seconds later, the straps slid down her shoulders and her breasts fell into his waiting hands. "Mmm, so good," he said. He cupped and stroked her, then bent to taste, and electric need ran instantly to her core.

There was something hugely erotic about being topless while he was still fully dressed, and they explored that for a long time, until finally she grew impatient and dealt with his black T-shirt almost as swiftly as he'd dealt with her red-and-green. His bare chest was silky and hot when she pressed her swollen breasts against him, and she couldn't stifle the moan that surfaced from deep within her.

"Bed?" he said.

"Yes."

They went through to it, stripping jeans and underwear and shoes on the way. There was no light on in the room, but it spilled through from the table lamps in her small living area in a soft shaft of gold. She liked the light, liked its softness, too. They could see each other, but not too clearly. They could see enough to discover that they were both smiling, not enough to see if the smiles faltered.

Because, you know, this couldn't help but feel a little scary.

"Now…" he murmured, and she stepped into the heat of his body space once more.

He cupped her backside, tracing its curve down to her thighs, his touch light and slow, and she closed her eyes and stood motionless for several long moments, giving herself completely to the male scent of his skin, mingled with coffee and spice and beer, giving herself to the touch of her naked body against his, the sound of his breathing, the warm press of his mouth on her neck and shoulder and the slopes of her breasts.

It was beautiful. That was the only way to describe it. Funny and heartfelt and beautiful. The way they fell onto the bed together, the way he propped himself on his elbows above her and showed her just how ready he was for this.

"Tell me what you want," he said softly.

"Nothing too fancy," she replied, trying to tease.

He took her seriously. "No?" He whispered kisses at the corners of her mouth as he spoke. "Not?"

"Why? You?"

What do you like, Mac?

"Not that fancy, either. Gotta leave room for improvement."

"We can start out pretty strong, even with nothing fancy."

"We can."

They grinned at each other in the low light. People called it "vanilla sex," and didn't mean that in a good way, but vanilla was a pretty popular flavor, after all. The feel of his weight poised over her, the hard heat of his body cradled in her opened thighs, the way she could hold him, wrap her arms all the way around and feel the strong, muscular cage of his chest. It was all so good, and it didn't need to be inventive.

They didn't need props or role play or gymnastics. Not tonight, anyhow. Not this first time.

Because she knew instinctively that it was going to be the *first,* not the *only,* and he seemed to know it, too.

He rolled her so that she was on top, and she arched upward to let him find her breasts again, with his hands and his mouth. He lavished them with hungry attention, cupping and stroking, covering her hardened nipples with his hot mouth. He lavished her with attention *everywhere,* in places she'd never thought of before. The creases between her arms and her body, the small of her back.

When he entered her, she was slick and swollen and ready, and the feel of him sliding against her had her whimpering and crying out so fast. It came out of nowhere. It came out of all those minutes and minutes of kissing.

But then he pulled back and swore, and it went away. "What did we forget?"

She understood, and swore, too. "I have some…"

"Good, because I don't."

"…as long as they're not expired."

"Hope they're not." He added after a moment, "And yet I'm sort of glad there's a chance they might be."

"Huh?" She was trying to reach for her bedside table drawer, but he wasn't letting her. He was pulling her back against him, trying to pillow her head against his shoulder. "You're *glad* they might be past their use-by date?"

"Yes, because I'm glad you… Well…" He hesitated, sounding gruff. "Hope you don't mind this, maybe it sounds too old-fashioned. I'm glad it doesn't happen like this for you all that often, I mean. Is that okay to say?"

"Of course, if it's the truth."

"We're all about plain sex and honesty?"

"Sounds good so far."

"Does," he agreed, still gruff.

"So is it okay for me to say I'm glad you don't carry them in your jacket wherever you go?"

"Haven't needed any for…probably six months." He thought a moment. "No, longer."

"Good to know." They lay there for a moment. "Although this whole discussion does seem like it might have killed the mood."

"Not letting anything kill the mood," he said.

"No?"

"I mean it! Find those suckers!"

She did. They were right in the bottom of her messy drawer, and they hadn't expired. There was still a whole week left on the clock.

"See?" he said when she told him.

"See what?"

"See how this was meant to happen?"

"Why, yes, now that you mention it, I do…."

So it didn't kill the mood, it simply changed it, and somehow they went from all that incredibly serious kissing in the kitchen, into a pillow fight kind of feeling. Getting the sheets and comforter into a tangle, pushing half the pillows onto the floor, laughing and chasing each other all over the bed until they were both breathless.

Until once again he was poised on top of her, looking down into her face with those dark eyes, his erection safely sheathed this time. She looked up at him, stroked the wave of thick dark brown hair away from his forehead, traced the lines of his parted lips with her fingertips and watched as he lowered himself and slid in, came back to the rhythm and push that had brought her so close so fast, before.

They never looked away. She hadn't known that it could be so intense, watching each other. Or so intimate. She gripped his back, wrapped her legs around him, as if their locked-together gaze was a taut thread that would break if she didn't hold on to him as hard as she could. In his face she could read the building of his release, and even at that moment they didn't break eye contact.

He pressed his lips tight together, closed his eyes for a fraction of a second—dark lashes sweeping down, then up—and the wave of his climax broke against her body while she panted for breath, then cried out and moaned against the sudden crush of his mouth on hers.

Neither of them spoke for a long while after they were still. She lay there with his body still flung over hers, her limbs encircling him, his softening heat still filling her. After a little while, he eased aside as if he could tell the moment he began to feel too heavy on her.

He touched her lightly and almost methodically, as if to check that everything was still there and whole, cupping each breast in turn, making patterns with his touch along her sides, down to her hips, running the flat of his hand over her stomach, resting his palm against the mound that felt so swollen and sensitized.

"Four seasons in one day, weren't we, do you think?" he said softly. "Like the weather in the mountains."

"We were, a bit," she agreed. "Which season is this?" She stretched and wriggled against him.

"Summer," he answered at once. "Warm and sleepy and happy. Sun on our skin."

"Mmm, I like summer. And winter."

"I like them all."

"Me, too. I like the point when it changes. First snowfall. First hint of fall. That tiny shift, but really the whole earth is turning."

"Yes, when you feel something new in the air, and you know it's just the start." Was he still talking about the seasons? She wasn't sure if she was.

Deliberately, she brought it back to concrete detail, instead of words that could have two meanings. "Love the snowmelt swelling the creeks and rivers."

"Love a hard frost turning the leaves in one night."

"And hiking through those deep drifts of gold and brown, when the air smells all peaty and fresh."

"You're a real outdoorsy gal."

"I am."

"Like that. Like my women athletic."

They talked, not saying anything very much, until they fell asleep.

Chapter Four

That was day one.

Christmas took over most of day two.

Lee awoke early in the morning to hear Mac calling his family in Idaho, standing in her kitchen and keeping his voice down. "C'mon, sis, I knew you'd be up with the kids," she heard him say.

Upstairs, the Narmans and their guests were up with the kids, too, and she knew she needed to touch base with them right away, to see what they wanted for cleaning and catering over the next few days. She called the cleaning company first, to confirm availability, using the boss's home number, and booked them in tentatively for eight this morning. It was only six-thirty now, but the cleaner was happy to hear from her. He could charge a mint for working on Christmas morning.

Lee jumped in the shower for a two-minute scrub and then dressed quickly. Mac was still on the phone. *"Doing my second job,"* she mouthed at him, pointing up at the ceiling. He nodded.

The Narmans were very happy about the cleaners coming at eight. Most of the party was still in bed, just two sets of bleary-looking parents in pajamas and robes up and about, watching their impatient, early rising kids dive into the contents of several bulging stockings.

"Catering, no, not for today," they told her. "You

filled the refrigerator with everything we needed for last night—thanks so much. And for Christmas dinner we're eating out."

They talked through a few more details—they wanted a four-course spread for twenty people catered for later in the week, and someone had broken the glass shower door in one of the bathrooms, so could she arrange to get that replaced? Then Lee did a quick collection of bottles and cans and empty pizza boxes, and took out four bags of trash.

She was taking the final bulging bag to the little wooden trash hut that kept out bears and raccoons when Mr. Narman, Sr., found her and presented her with a list of eight more "little details" that needed her attention. More shopping, another repair job, reservations at various restaurants to make on their behalf and several more items.

"Is it always like this when they're around?" Mac asked, when she told him she would probably be tied up most of the day, and then there was her dinner with friends to go to. She'd made coffee, and pointed to the cereal packets and the toaster and the bread.

"Pretty much. But they're polite about it, and it's such a good arrangement for me. Very cozy when they're not around and I get to go upstairs."

"Oh, you get to use the house?"

"Yep." She grinned. "Laze in front of the open fire and drink champagne in the Jacuzzi." She kicked off her boots and stretched her neck and shoulders in preparation for diving into all those phone calls.

"You were a cat in your previous life, I can tell."

"Oh, you can?"

"The way you stretched and purred when you said

that. The way you're just slightly trying to get rid of me because I'm crowding your space."

"Trying to—?"

Maybe I am.

He was grinning at her, leaning on an elbow in the kitchen doorway, with their breakfast dishes—two mugs, two plates—sitting in the sink behind him. The accusation hadn't been made in anger. "It's okay," he said. "I have stuff I need to do, too."

"I'm really not… I'm not pushing you out the door." She felt a little panicky that he'd read her so clearly, and that she'd given the wrong impression about last night.

"It's okay." It must be, because he was still grinning.

"It was…" She scrambled for the right words. So she was a cat. Did he *like* cats? "I loved it. I loved the whole night. Sleeping beside you. And then you were still here in the morning, and that was lovely, too. It really was."

"It's okay," he repeated patiently.

"I want to see you again," she blurted out, and then bit her lip, because maybe she'd overstated her case, maybe his recognition that she was ready for some alone time had made her too honest about how much she'd liked last night.

Damn!

Or not.

He was smiling. Again. "So do I. Soon. We can make a plan now, if you want. Or if you don't know when you'll next revert from feline to human form, we can leave it and make a plan later."

"Now. We can make a plan now. I'm only a cat some of the time."

"Aha, is that a confession?" He stepped toward her and swung her easily into his arms, lacing his fingers in the small of her back and rocking her from side to side. It was as if they were dancing. "I knew it! I knew you were a cat."

"Do you, um, like them?"

"Like what?"

"Cats."

"What's not to like?" he said softly. "They feel good to touch." He ran his hand down the side seam of her jeans. "And if you treat them right, they purr for you." He brushed the skin behind her ears and under her jaw, and so help her, she almost did purr! Her eyes wanted to close, and she wanted to rub against him and coil up and stay there. And she'd most definitely purred last night. But there were things to do and places to be....

He was still speaking. She opened her eyes again and found him looking at her. "And their eyes go big when something exciting happens."

"Yours, too," she whispered. Big and so dark.

"And they're such phenomenal athletes, so fit and sinuous, the way they move. They know how to use their bodies so well. I've always loved that in a...cat."

He was speaking of her, not cats at all, but all she could think of was him. She could imagine him, suddenly, out on a powder run, making effortless, snaking tracks through pristine snow with his shoulders squared to the slope and his strong legs pumping like pistons or springs.

"Let's ski together," she blurted out. "Could that be part of the plan? For next time?"

"And sometimes they're just plain hilarious."

"Wh—?"

"I'm seducing you, Lee, and you want to hit the slopes."

"No, I..."

Shoot, how did I miss that? Of course he's seducing me!

"We have time," he insisted.

"Do we?"

"If we're fast. And not fancy." He added slyly, "I'll set my watch."

She laughed. "How long?"

"Ten minutes. Fifteen, by the time our shoes are back on."

"You're serious."

"I totally am."

So they were fast and not fancy, stripping and laughing and falling on the bed, and taking every shortcut they could think of....

Oh, it was so good. So short, but so hot and good. She knew they would both be laughing about it, thinking back. Laughing about the fact that you could make it into a race and still get it right.

The timer on his watch started bleeping just as he was reaching for his socks. "Damn! We didn't make it as far as the shoes!" he said.

"Near enough," she suggested.

"Near enough is not good enough. We'll have to go for a rematch on this one."

"On the fast thing?"

"Why, didn't you like that?"

"I did," she said.

With a look of lascivious reminiscence, he drawled at her, "Yeah, you did."

Oh, she did, she liked it! Mac enjoyed the memories in this area whenever they wandered through his mind that day—and it was often.

He didn't see any point in pretending about this kind

of thing. He felt what he felt, and he let it show. He never made promises he didn't intend to keep. Most of the time, this meant not making any promises at all. Better safe than sorry. She seemed to be the same, the kind of woman who played it straight, who wasn't about games or emotional blackmail or saying one thing when she meant the opposite.

He hadn't come to Aspen with the idea of hooking up with someone right away, and was a little surprised, to be honest, that it had happened like this.

Well, huh. So he had a woman in his bed, and it seemed to be working.

Nice.

All the same, from the word *go,* he kept a good lookout for danger signs and deal breakers, because even the most apparently casual fling could have a sting in the tail if you weren't careful….

Lee didn't mention Mac to her friends at Christmas dinner that night, but then she saw him every day for a week. He found a small apartment down valley, about twenty minutes' drive, but told her, "You're not seeing it until I have it fixed up a little," so they always came back to her place. He downloaded and read *A Room of One's Own,* on his eReader, "Purely so I can drink from more of your mugs." She told him he was an idiot, and it became a running joke between them.

The Narmans left the day after New Year's, which gave Lee a full schedule of instructing all day and then cleaning the house out until past eleven o'clock that night, with more still to do the next day. It was only when the Narmans were in residence that she called in the team of cleaners, who could be in and out in an hour. When the family wasn't around, she did the work herself, because then it didn't matter if it took her a day or two, and she could make sure it was done absolutely right.

But there was no time for Mac.

Two days later, when she'd closed the doors of all the spare bedrooms, replenished supplies and sent several things off to the dry cleaners, she grabbed a private moment with him at the ski school office and told him, "Guess what? We can have the house today."

"The whole house?"

"Well, I usually just stick to one bedroom and bathroom, but, yep, they're not due back until three days at the end of January."

"Will we be able to find each other in that place?" He gave her a big grin. "Should we text our whereabouts whenever we move rooms?"

"We could get one of those Swiss alpenhorns that are about eight feet long."

"Or walkie-talkies."

"Or a 1970s intercom system."

Another instructor overheard them. "Oh, wow, my house used to have one of those! My parents tortured us with it." He gave a chuckle and shook his head. "We had Muzak piped into every room." He moved on, out of earshot.

"Lucky we weren't talking about various other possible subjects," Mac muttered in Lee's ear.

"I'm ready to talk about them tonight," she muttered back.

"When?"

"Whenever."

Having the whole house turned them both into kids in a candy store. Mac went shopping and came back with champagne, smoked salmon, caviar and anything else that had caught his eye and said *luxury*. Lee filled the Jacuzzi and lit the fire. They closed the drapes, which the Narmans always seemed to prefer open, even though the curtains moved back and forth at the touch of an electronic button.

"Can we have music?" Mac asked.

"Go for it."

He strode into the side room where there was a huge bank of audio equipment, and put on a rock compilation CD. "They really don't mind you doing this?" he said when he came back into the kitchen.

"They ask for it specifically. They hate if the place looks dark and unattended. The lights in my little cubbyhole don't show from the street, or from the slopes."

"How did you get this gig, anyhow?"

"I taught some of them to ski, they started asking for me for private lessons every time they came, and it went from there. The girl I was sharing with down valley got a boyfriend and wanted him to move in. There wasn't room for three of us. Mr. Narman was looking for a live-in janitor. The timing was right, and it's worked out really well. I've been doing it several years now."

"It definitely has worked well. I think this caviar plan of mine is going to work out pretty well, too." He thumped the side of the jar lid on a wooden cutting board to break the seal, and twisted it open. "My only question is whether we eat in the Jacuzzi or by the fire."

"From experience, I can tell you that eating in the Jacuzzi isn't all it's cracked up to be. Things end up floating and getting on your skin, and caviar is not my favorite flavor in a moisturizer." She pulled a chilled bottle out of the shopping bag. "Champagne in the Jacuzzi, on the other hand…"

So they drank champagne there, using the very nice

plastic picnic champagne flutes the Narmans kept for the purpose.

"They're pretty fussy about the possibility of broken glass," Lee explained. She lay back in the foaming water, letting the jets bounce her gently and keep her afloat.

Mac did the same on the opposite side of the vast tub. "I can see why they like you. You keep to their rules even when they're not here."

"They're nice people, despite being a touch over-the-top."

"Why are you all the way over there, by the way?"

"Because I had to pour the champagne, and it's sitting right behind me."

"But now you've poured the champagne, and the distance is a problem."

"What, you think we need the alpenhorn to communicate?"

"I just want you here." He moved forward a little and held out his arm, and she went to him, sliding against him all slick and slippery with the foam, and he wrapped an arm around her bare, foamy wet butt to keep her in place, and it felt so sexy and good. "You're so beautiful, Lee…."

"Me?" People didn't say that about her. They said she had a strong face, a melodic voice, an athlete's body, great hair. They said she was striking, or pretty—which was a real stretch, because she knew her face was way too strong for *pretty*.

"You're beautiful," he repeated. "Your eyes. Can't decide if they're blue or green. Your smile. So much life. The way you laugh is beautiful. Your mouth, all lush. The way you threw your head around with those earrings, first time I saw you."

"Yeah?" She floated against him, pressed nose to nose and stole some kisses.

"That did it for me. I saw you, the way your hair bounced, dark gold and a little messy, and you had this look on your face."

"And we talked as if we already knew each other."

"It felt like we did. And now we really do." He hiked her hips against his so she could feel what she was doing to him.

"We really do…." she whispered.

What happened next was fairly predictable.

What happened next had been happening a lot.

Still new.

Different every time.

Amazing every time.

That night, he stayed over, but he didn't always. As the days went by, they both seemed to know when it was time for a little extra space. Mac needed to set up his new apartment. Lee had some heavy days of coaching junior racers, ahead of a competition tour to Europe that they were taking in February.

"February?" Mac said when she told him. "When in February?"

"We leave on the third."

"The third, and you're only just telling me?"

"I wasn't *not* telling you. People are talking about it. I thought you might have heard."

"Hmm. Well, I hadn't."

"Sorry."

"No biggie. You're telling me now. So you'll be away how long?"

"Three weeks."

"That long?"

"It's a new thing we're trying this season. Hand-picked group, a little younger than usual."

"Hope you have some parents going."

"We do. I'm not organizing that side of it."

"What happens with this place?"

They were both sprawled on the sheepskin rug in front of the open fire, having this conversation, eating cheese and crackers and drinking red wine. It was late January by this time, the Narmans were due for a three-day weekend, and Lee was startled when she did a mental calculation and realized she and Mac had been seeing each other—involved…together…whatever this was called—for over a month.

It wasn't called anything. They didn't have a name for it, or an end-date for it, or anything like that. They were careful about it. Maybe more careful than when it had first started. The times they spent together were more intense, and yet at the same time more relaxed. The times they were apart…

Well, Lee was starting to need those, so she made sure they were more frequent.

Because if she didn't have them, she began to get scared about the questions in her head. You could get yourself into a lot of trouble if you were with someone for the wrong reasons.

Right now, she dragged herself back to Mac's question, instead. "What happens with this place is that my friend Alyssa moves in. She's done it before, and the Narmans like her, too. I'm sure if I ever give this up, she'll take over. She's a little younger than me, twenty-nine, similar in a lot of ways. Single and planning to stay that way."

He didn't comment on that last bit. Hearing it play back in her head, she thought it sounded too abrupt, like a warning. If she could have a do-over, she would have softened it a little. *Alyssa* was the one who was single and planning to stay that way.

Me, I'm not set in stone about it. That's not the way we're similar.

"So where are you going?" Mac said, after a moment. "Where in Europe, I mean."

"Oh, Val d'Isère, Chamonix, Sestriere, a couple of other places."

"Pretty hectic."

"It will be."

"Are you looking forward to it?"

"I think so."

"I'll miss you."

"I'll miss you."

He sat up on his elbow, coming dangerously close to hitting the glass of wine. "You're allowed to say it differently, you know. You don't have to choose the exact same words that I did."

"I was happy with your word choice." She dived in and rescued the glass, before he knocked it with his elbow and ruined the rug. Then she stayed close to him, because it was always, always nice to be close to him.

"I'll try to be more creative next time," he drawled.

"I said I was happy with it," she pointed out, distracted by what the drawl did to the shape of his mouth. It made it better, and it was pretty shapely to begin with.

"Happy isn't good enough. I'm going for *happier*. I like to win, remember? Haven't we discussed this?" Now the mouth was tilted up at one corner, inviting her to kiss it straight.

"We have," she answered solemnly. "I like to win, too."

"So you should have tried to outdo me. I'll miss you. You'll miss me wildly." Now he was openly smiling.

She couldn't stop herself from grinning back. "I'll miss you wildly, Mac."

She was a little afraid that it was true.

He leaned toward her. Her action with the wineglass had brought her well within reach—a place she was very happy to be. "Much better. Wildly. I like it. You said it with such feeling, too."

"I'll miss you madly. Excruciatingly. Hopelessly."

"Not hopelessly. It's only three weeks. But keep trying." He rolled an inch or two, and his chest weighed against her side.

"I'll miss you with every fiber of my being." She touched his upper arm, where he had a really nice hard muscle that she could never resist.

"Still room for improvement."

"Yeah, really?"

"You gotta show it, not tell it. Better get some practice." She knew that look. He was about to kiss her. Good! She nestled closer, to make it easy for him. "There'll be a test on this material next week," he warned.

"Next week, I think I'll be in Zermatt."

Chapter Five

Next week was still several days away. Or rather, several nights. Mac spent three of those nights at her place, and they had lunch together twice, both times at the top of the mountain, where everything was overpriced and not that good for you.

"Shall we watch the snowboarding while we eat our giant hot dogs?" Lee suggested on their last day together. He wasn't staying over tonight, because she and the squad were flying out early tomorrow.

"Sure. What is it?"

"Men's Superpipe Elimination."

"Those guys are crazy."

"Says the man who told me in bed the other night that it was 'fun' skiing through an avalanche."

"Yeah, but that was a double-edged 'fun.' You do know that, right? I was being all manly and tough. At the time it was pretty scary."

"These guys get scared."

"They like that. I don't."

"No?"

"I'm all about risk minimization."

"They wear helmets."

"Not good enough." Mac gave a quick smile, but there was an edge to the words all the same. Some people had a fierce loyalty to their own preferred winter sports, and were very dismissive of everything else. Mac was a skier, not a boarder. She put it down to that, and forgave him for it. It wasn't all that important, since she wasn't a boarder herself.

"Hey, I just thought it might be nice to watch some impressive rides, instead of sitting in that crowded place. But if you don't want to…" she offered.

"No, it's fine. Really. You're right, they're impressive."

They put on their skis and stuffed their wrapped hot dogs into the fronts of their jackets to keep them warm while they skied a hundred meters down the hill. There wasn't a huge crowd for this round of the competition, so they found a good vantage point close to the action and ate standing up with skis on.

Mary Jane and Daisy thought their middle sister was crazy to love a life that contained moments like these, but Lee did love it—loved the clean air, loved the feel of having a fit body, loved the rawness of the whole experience…and then the bliss of a hot bath or an open fire, and curling up with a book before sleeping like a log.

Today, even the hot dog wasn't bad.

The spectators whooped at the tricks and the height, while the commentator reeled off the moves. "Cab 7… Frontside 1080… Double alley-oop rodeo—wow, that's been tried in competition only a handful of times—but doesn't nail the landing… Backside 9… Frontside 5…"

Lee whooped a little bit, also, in between bites of gluey bread, rubbery hot dog and dripping ketchup. The boarders shot ten or fifteen feet in the air above the lip of the pipe and swooped back down. Mac didn't whoop, just hissed in a breath every now and then, or said, "Whoa!"

"I know," she agreed, after a massive backside 1080, nailed perfectly.

"They weren't doing stuff like this a few years ago, were they?"

"No, they get better every year. You never watch X Games comps?"

"Nah, not really. Not my thing."

"Sorry, then."

"No." He turned to her, frowning. "Don't apologize. Just personal preference, okay? If you like it, it's fine. We're not joined at the hip. Which is…convenient, right?" He did that thing with his eyes that she loved, sweeping a look down her body and then back up, mentally stripping her, claiming her with the glint of his smile.

"Very convenient. Or we'd have to be double-jointed or something. You have ketchup on your face. Right at the corner of your mouth."

"Wanna get it off?"

So they missed an especially impressive frontside inverted 7, and Lee decided maybe Mac was right, watching snowboarding didn't rate with certain other lunchtime treats. When it was time to head down to pick up their classes for the afternoon, he told her, "Text me from Zermatt," and they parted with Lee feeling incredibly happy and lucky that they'd met.

Zermatt, Sestriere, Claviere, Chamonix, Val d'Isère…

The kids had a great time, and their ski racing skills improved by leaps and bounds, with the challenge of new terrain and varied conditions. Most of them were well-behaved, and the two sets of parents who'd accompanied the team provided very helpful discipline to support Lee and senior coach Everard.

But it was exhausting.

Lee fell into bed every night and disappeared into a black hole of deep sleep, and sometimes when she woke up, she couldn't remember what country she was in, or what day it was. She'd bought a cheap European phone with prepaid credit so she and Mac could speak to each other without racking up huge charges, but they ended up mostly texting, because they never seemed to be free to talk—or awake—at the same time.

By the time she'd reached Geneva airport for the flight home, she had to tell him, via text as usual, Home around nine tonight Colorado time, but will need a couple of days.

She had to turn her phone off during the flight, and didn't see his answering text until they landed in Denver. No problem. We've discussed this before remember I like you awake.

For the next week, jet lag pulled Lee awake at some strange times, and Mac didn't seem to mind if she woke him up, too. At three in the morning, by stealthily running her hands over his body until he stirred and then sighed and then rolled over and grabbed her and groaned and buried his face in her hair. At four in the morning, by spooning him from behind and kissing the warmth of his neck and shoulder. At five in the morning, by simply whispering to him, "Mac, are you awake?"

"I am now."

"Are you happy to be?"

"Depends what you're offering…."

"Well, the usual."

"Then I'm happy."

She'd been back for ten days when it was his turn to be away. He had an interview scheduled, at short notice, for a management position at Barrier Mountain in Idaho, and had decided to spend a few days with his family while he was up there.

"Are you hoping to move back to Idaho?" Lee asked him, when he told her about the interview and the extension to his trip. They were grabbing lunch in the usual huge, noisy place at the top of the mountain, where the floor was wet with snowmelt from skiers' boots and the menu had less sophistication than a roadside diner.

"I'll go where there's a good job. This one came up very fast."

"What's your definition of a good job?"

"Permanent, year-round, in a nice town, with scope for really achieving something. Ecotourism, new snow sports, better summer programs, on-the-ball risk management. But if I can get something in Idaho, yes, I guess that's a plus." Someone bumped his chair while threading between the tables and gave a quick apology.

"So you like your family," Lee said.

"I do." He shifted his chair a little closer to the table, bringing them within easier range for this conversation, which had turned far too serious for a fifteen-minute lunch between ski classes. "How about you? Would you ever move from Aspen? Move back east?"

It shocked her.

Not so much the question, but her own response. "I've always assumed not."

"So you *don't* like your family."

"No, I do. A lot."

But I like my space, too.

She liked her space *more?*

He looked at her as if he was waiting for something. A "but."

I like my family, but they don't understand me.

I like my family, but they drive me crazy after two days.

I like my family, but I love *my independence. I never want to lose sight of who I am. I always want to be sure about what I'm doing, and why I'm doing it.*

"So?" Mac prompted.

"I don't know," she said. "If there was a reason to move back…"

"Like one of your parents was ill, or something?"

"My parents have just moved to South Carolina. But, yes, that kind of a reason."

Someone else bumped into them—Lee's chair this time. They'd finished their burgers and their break was almost over.

It had begun to snow thick, dry flakes that would bring visibility down to near zero and make teaching a challenge. Outside, in the midst of the silent, half-suffocating fall, Mac planted a quick, cold kiss on her mouth and they trapped fluffy flakes between their bodies. It was too cold for the flakes to melt.

"See you when I get back," he told her.

"Talk to you before that."

"Yes."

They put on their skis, waved at each other and went separate ways.

That night, via a thought process that started with the calendar and the fact that she would miss him for the next four days, and then jumped through several more steps, it finally occurred to Lee that she hadn't had her period in a while.

"Not to panic about it, or anything," she told the Narmans' enormous two-door refrigerator—because yes, she still spoke aloud to an empty room when Mac wasn't around.

She leaned her elbows on the granite counter and

thought it through. Should have happened in Sestriere. Or possibly Chamonix.

Three weeks late.

She was so out of the habit of thinking about things like this. She'd never noted dates on the calendar, being somewhat irregular and always getting plenty of warning rather than a potentially embarrassing flood. When it started, she always thought, *Oh. Right,* and took the necessary action.

Three weeks.

And it was currently nine o'clock at night.

She wasn't having any noticeable symptoms, either premenstrual or pregnancy, so there was no guide in that department. She decided to worry about it in the morning, if nothing had happened.

In the morning, nothing had.

She decided to pick up a test on the way home that night. She had no idea how they worked. Something involving pee and plastic sticks, pink lines or blue crosses, or something. It took her a while even to locate them in the drugstore aisle, and then there seemed to be a bewildering array of brands, each promising a faster process and a more accurate result than the last.

She chose one eventually. Didn't do that thing women always seemed to do on TV, of buying a whole boxful of tests and taking them all in succession. One was enough. Lee felt as if this was a game more than reality, and she was relieved to see that a young girl she didn't know was working the checkout counter. Also relieved that Mac was up in Idaho, so she didn't have to hide this silliness from him.

Or reveal it.

She honestly expected to find that her period had started before she even took the test out of the box.

It hadn't.

Which probably meant she should move from Step One, Buying the Test, to Step Two, Taking It.

"I'll be laughing about this in five minutes."

Well, laughing on the other side of her face, as it turned out.

"What does that even mean?" she asked her reflection in the Narmans' ornate bathroom mirror, with the plastic stick still in her hand, bearing its two pink lines.

Then she really did laugh, because this didn't feel real or believable or even possible, and maybe that was why she was talking to herself more than usual. It was the sixth of March. She'd known Mac for ten weeks and now she was having his baby.

The idea sat in front of her like an ornate cake she hadn't yet cut into, and had no idea where to start, or whether she even liked cake.

She dropped the test in the bathroom wastebasket and wandered out of the room and through the house, glad of its vastness.

This wasn't real yet.

Not at all.

And the only thing she could think right now was, *Thank heaven Mac is away. Thank heaven I'm not seeing him till Sunday.*

And that was wrong, wasn't it? Shouldn't she want him here? Wouldn't any normal woman be in floods of tears because he wasn't?

But his absence gave her time, and that was good.

Time for this to sink in. Time for it to turn into something that was really, actually happening to her, instead of being like some kind of dream state, like taking a vacation in someone else's body, someone else's life. This wasn't *her*.

She had four days to find out where this fitted into her life, to become herself again—or a new version of herself—and decide what she was going to do, and make sure it was the best decision possible.

"You sure you don't want something to eat before you go out?" Mac's mother said to him.

She ran water over a pile of potatoes to wash off the dirt, her hair scraped out of the way in a high ponytail that somehow suited her even though she was in her late fifties now. There were silver threads in the ponytail, but still a lot of black, and she was proud of that. "If I dyed it," he'd heard her say, "everyone would think I was totally gray underneath, but I'm not very gray at all, and I want people to know it!"

It was five-thirty on Saturday evening, and he was sitting at the kitchen table in his childhood home, while his mother made dinner for herself and his dad and his sister, Lisa, and her family, who were coming over.

Mac had already seen Lisa and Andy and the kids last night, when they'd all gone out for a meal, and this morning he'd gone to watch nine-year-old Liam's ice hockey game, so he didn't plan on spending the evening with them tonight. He was seeing a bunch of his old friends instead.

Still, they were great kids, Liam and five-year-old Krista, and he got on just as well with Lisa and Andy. It would be nice to have another family meal before he flew back to Colorado tomorrow, even if it was short. "I guess the guys aren't picking me up until seven." He suspected they had a heavy night in mind, too, and doubted he'd get in again before midnight. "What time are you planning to eat?"

"Oh, we'll eat at six or six-fifteen. The kids are always starving by then. They'll be here any moment."

"I'll have something with you, then. I can save room for more later with the guys."

"It's good that you're getting a chance to catch up with them."

"Might be moving back pretty close to here, if the job comes through."

"Would you? Are you seriously considering it?" Her face lit up.

"Don't get excited. Really, Mom. I shouldn't have even told you that's why I'm up here."

"I thought you were settled in Utah. Next thing I know you're in Colorado, and now you're thinking about another move."

"Is that a loaded observation?"

"Well…just wondering."

"Wondering what?"

"Did the whole…?" She stopped. "Did Sloane…?" She stopped again. "Did what happened with her stop you from ever wanting…?"

He hated when his mother brought up the subject, but to her credit, she knew that—hence the hesitation—and didn't do it often. "I don't know," he answered truthfully. "I seriously don't know, Mom."

An image of Lee flashed into his mind and he had to fight to stop himself from grinning. They'd texted a couple of times, but hadn't talked. He liked that she never crowded him, never asked for more than he wanted to give. In fact, she seemed even more independent than he was, in some ways.

Was there a future in what they had?

He didn't see the need to ask himself that yet, and apparently Lee didn't, either. Even if the job came through here in Idaho, and even if he decided to take it, he wouldn't be starting for another couple months. There would be time at that point for them both to think about whether they wanted to say goodbye or try for something longer and stronger.

"I wish you could tell me," his mother said wistfully, in response to his inadequate answer.

"I know you do. But how can I? Maybe it's the kind of bridge I can only cross if I get to it."

"And no bridges visible on the road ahead?"

"Don't think so." He added, after a moment, "I've been seeing someone, but I don't think it's serious." He said *"don't think"* instead of *"don't know if"* quite deliberately, so that Mom wouldn't get her hopes up. But she was hopeful by nature, so his careful word choice didn't really help.

"You didn't think it was serious with Sloane."

"And it wasn't," he answered.

"She was having—"

He cut her off quickly. "Yes, and that was a mistake, and it was the *only* reason we were together, in the end. And we weren't even really together."

His mother sighed. She'd come of age in the early seventies, when the boundaries and rules in relationships had begun to lose the rigidity of earlier generations, but still, she and his dad had been married for thirty-six years. She believed in monogamy and commitment and pretty weddings, and Mac could see her biting her tongue sometimes, to stop herself from begging him to do it properly.

Find the right girl, marry her, start a family.

If anything, Dad was even worse.

"Be careful, Mac, won't you?" she said, the same way she and his dad always did.

"I will," he promised her, without having the slightest idea how to do that. Careful? Get Lee to fill in a questionnaire about her attitudes?

He heard the ring tone on his phone, coming from the couch in the living room where he'd put it down. He went and grabbed it before it switched to voice mail, and heard his friend Sam. "Hey, Mac, you want to make it earlier tonight? Brandon's done with his game. He just called and he's already at the bar, so I thought I'd head on over. Shall I swing by for you?"

"Yeah, do that, that'd be good," he said.

"See you in ten."

He put the phone in his pocket and went back into the kitchen. "Change of plan. Sam's picking me up early."

"Oh, so you won't eat with us, after all." Mom's disappointment was clear.

"Sorry." But he wasn't, at heart. He didn't want any more difficult questions about how he felt about the past or what he planned for the future, and if Mom was in this kind of a mood, she might not have the willpower to stop asking.

Mac seemed really happy to see her when he got back from Idaho. Lee liked that about him. He didn't pretend. He didn't use his emotions as a power play or a way of keeping her guessing. When he was happy, it showed. When he was bored, it showed. When he was tired, same thing.

He arrived in the evening, having flown from Spokane via Seattle to Denver, where he'd left his pickup in the long-stay airport parking four days ago. He sent her a text about an hour before he got in. In at eight. Too late to see you?

She texted back, Eight is fine, then wondered why

she hadn't given herself more time. She could have put him off until tomorrow. She'd made her decisions and had no real reason to think he wouldn't be happy about them—he might even be relieved—but the thought of talking about them scared her, all the same.

How did you say something like this? Was it better or worse that there were friends of the Narmans using the house for an extended weekend, so she was back in her little cat nest of an apartment? There was so little room in here for all the emotion that might soon be flying around....

At her door, he started smiling as soon as he saw her. He heaved his bag inside, then crushed her in his arms. "I'm wiped," he announced. "So good to be back. Ton of stuff to tell you and talk about."

"So good to see you. Very, very good. Stuff to talk about, too." She stretched up and rubbed her cheek against his before turning into the kiss he had waiting for her, a big, hearty, sexy one, with one of those rumbling, satisfied sounds that came from deep within his broad chest.

The smell of his skin was so delicious she wanted to stay like this for the rest of the evening. Not even undress or make love or talk or anything, just stay like this, wrapped in his arms, smelling his familiar scent, feeling the strength and the warmth, feeling wanted.

Would he guess that there was something going on? She was jittery and emotional and unsettled, and despite the picture she'd created for her future with the baby, it still didn't seem as if it was really happening.

Pregnant. A baby.

Should she have waited? Should she have held herself in limbo and not made any decisions at all until she'd sounded him out?

I won't tell him tonight. He says he's tired....

"Hungry, too?" she asked, letting go a little. To have decided that she wouldn't be having a big, fat, important conversation tonight felt like a huge reprieve.

"I should have stopped for something."

"But you didn't."

"I missed an exit near the airport where there were a whole lot of fast-food places, couldn't be bothered to turn around and go back. Passed a few other possibilities, but decided to drive straight through."

"So you haven't eaten since…?"

"Tiny bag of crackers and some pop on the plane. Hours ago." It was a four-hour drive from the Denver airport.

"Bacon and eggs?"

"You're wonderful."

She went through to the kitchen and opened the refrigerator, while he slumped on the couch. "Did you have a good time with your family?" she asked him.

I'm pregnant, Mac.

"I had a great time. And last night, with friends. Bit too great a time. Didn't get to bed until three, and then I was up at six. My dad drove me to Spokane for my flight, and he likes to allow plenty of time. Then the flight out of Seattle was late."

"This is why you're tired."

I'm pregnant. This is why I'm *tired, and my breasts are starting to get sore.*

"It is."

"Any news about the job at Barrier Mountain?"

"Nothing yet. They said it would be sometime this week."

"But you thought the interview went well?"

"You never really know, do you? But, yeah, I did.

That's what I want to tell you about. The people seemed great. They have some big ideas about what they want to do on the mountain, and they wanted my ideas, too. It would be a step up. If I get it. If I take it. More ambitious than anything I've done before, but they could see I had the qualifications. I honestly did have a very good feeling about it. Just to have them offer it to me would feel good."

"That's great. I hope you hear soon."

"Me, too."

I'm pregnant, and you might be moving back to Idaho.

"How do you want your eggs? Scrambled? Fried?"

"Whatever's easiest. Need some help?"

"Not if you've had three hours of sleep." *And if you've had three hours of sleep, I'm definitely not going to talk about anything important tonight.* "I'll scramble them. How many?"

"Oh, six? Seven? Twelve?"

She laughed. "Make a decision. But I have to warn you, I don't have twelve."

"Four. And three slices of toast. And six pieces of bacon. I really have not eaten today."

"Four eggs I have. And I can fry some tomato, too, if you want it."

"Sounds great." He closed his eyes, and she had to stand in the kitchen doorway and watch him for a moment before she got to work. He looked so good, his body hard with muscle inside its black T-shirt, even when he was flopped on her couch like a rag doll, the planes of his face smooth and motionless, with his dark lashes thick against his tanned skin.

In one of their sleepy bedtime conversations, she'd asked him where he got the dark eyes and olive skin,

and he'd told her about his Spanish Basque grand-
mother, and his Italian great-grandfather who'd somehow ended up in Idaho in the early nineteen hundreds,
working for the railroad in Pocatello. "Both of them on
my mother's side."

"Which explains why you're called Wheeler, not
something cool and exotically European."

"Sadly, there is nothing cool and exotic about me,"
he'd said.

But he was wrong. Looking at him now, she felt that
same kick she'd felt the night they'd met. He did something to her, and they'd known each other only a couple
of months, and she hadn't been looking for anything
serious, and she didn't think he was, either, but he *did*
something to her, and she didn't know what that meant.

"So you would definitely take the job?" she asked
abruptly, and he opened his sleepy eyes and looked at
her, his face soft with fatigue. There were little creases
on his eyelids, above those gypsy-black eyes, and for a
few seconds she couldn't breathe.

"Cross that bridge when I come to it."

"That's not an answer."

"Because I haven't decided. Really tempted. But I
haven't been in Aspen long."

"So it should be easy to leave."

*Will it be easy for me to leave? I've been here for
years.*

"Or it makes me feel too much like a nomad to be
leaving again already."

"Not if you're leaving to go home."

"True." He yawned. "But if something in mountain
management came up here…" He looked at her, with
a sudden alertness that belied the yawn. "What do you
think about it?"

"I think I'd better make those eggs before you fall asleep completely."

"Fair point."

She had the meal ready for him in five minutes, and he ate it about that fast, too. He was in bed by nine, and she slid in beside him shortly afterward, and they snuggled against each other like furry animals keeping warm in a burrow, but he was asleep before they could even think about making love.

That was okay.

That was good, really, because if he'd been awake enough for lovemaking, he would have been awake enough for a talk, and she felt sick about the talk. She wasn't ready for it yet.

She held on to him, feeling the rise and fall of his chest as he breathed, feeling the wall of his body against her, feeling the squirmy sensation in her heart.

The next day at lunch, he told her, "I'm taking a pass tonight, if that's okay."

"Taking a pass?"

"On seeing you. I'm actually going home to my place and doing nothing but watch TV. I partied too hard in Idaho."

The statement bothered her on two levels. First, that he took it for granted she'd want to see him, and therefore needed to apologize as if he was letting her down. Second, the party thing. He was new in town, he might not be staying long and apparently he had a taste for the party-hard bachelor social life that he hadn't revealed before.

"So you have a split personality," she teased, hiding what she felt. "You're not a party animal here."

He shrugged and gave a rueful smile. "Just some friends I hadn't seen for a while. They led me astray."

"The truth about last night and all the bacon and eggs. You were still hungover."

"Well…maybe a bit. Candle burned at both ends, more like. Mind buzzing about the job at Barrier Mountain. The bacon and eggs were excellent, thank you. I may not have stressed that enough."

She'd apparently telegraphed that he did need to apologize, and this was what he'd fixed on.

I've made the right decision. I might be ready to be pregnant…just…but we're definitely not ready to do this together, to join our whole lives. We'd be doing it for all the wrong reasons.

And he'd given her another day's reprieve in the daunting task of talking about it. The relief and frustration she felt about this were yet more scary emotions in what was rapidly becoming a whole head and heart and gut full of them.

When some of her friends hauled her off to their table to share a pizza, while Everard and a couple of other guys in the line waiting to order a meal started talking to Mac about basketball, she let the separation happen without more than a quick finger-wave goodbye, but maybe that was wrong. Maybe it was cowardice.

She should have pushed for some private time.

Mac loved the way Lee wrinkled her nose like that, when she wasn't totally happy. Her finger-wave and her twinkling eyes and her body movement all said, "They want me to share their pizza, what can I say?" and only that little crimp in her nose told a different story.

Would rather be with you.

Same back at you, Lee, except I know I'll be a bear

with a sore head tonight. And right now I really, really don't feel like talking about basketball. Did that for about four hours on Saturday.

"Northwestern is going down, I'm telling you," someone said.

"Michigan."

"Are you kidding me?"

The words faded to a vague babble as he ate his burger.

Maybe they should see each other tonight, after all? Lee could come down to his place. She'd done that only a few times, because, really, why would you make that drive down valley when you had a mansion right on the mountain? Tonight, though… They could grab some takeout to eat while he threw his laundry into the machine, and she could go home early, and he'd get to see her but still feel as if he'd caught up a little on overdue chores and sleep.

He let the basketball talk wash over him, and didn't make any kind of decision about tonight, and next time he looked at her table, she'd already gone. He taught two challenging beginner group classes in the afternoon, full of guys who thought they were naturals and women who had no self-belief at all, and if the two sexes could just have met in the middle with their confidence levels, he wouldn't have had nearly as many spills and crashes to deal with.

He drove down the mountain at the end of the day, and his apartment seemed…well, a little pointless, really. Cramped bachelor pad with no charm, and the art photography he'd put on the walls wasn't enough. Thinking that Lee might be here—if he called her—he changed the sheets, did laundry and passed the vacuum cleaner, by which time it was after six.

Should he call her?

He pulled out his phone and came so close, thinking of the little wrinkle in her nose that said she wasn't quite as independent as he might have thought, thinking of talking to her more seriously about Idaho, about whether he should make the move, if he got an offer. Did they have the kind of relationship where they needed to consider each other before they made decisions or plans?

He should talk to her.

But not yet.

The thought of framing the words made him feel the fatigue in his limbs and the partied-too-hard heaviness in his head that still hadn't quite gone.

Leave it, he decided. See her tomorrow, when he could do it justice.

Chapter Six

That night Lee called Mr. Narman and told him she was moving out, because she really needed to let him know this as soon as possible. Whatever happened when she talked to Mac, she didn't intend to stay on here through a pregnancy and birth.

Mr. Narman cut very quickly to what was important from his end. "Would that friend of yours be interested in replacing you?"

"I hope so. I'm pretty sure."

"Sound her out. We've been happy when she's subbed for you. Tell her we'd offer the same arrangement. Can I trust you to fix it up, and get back to me if there's any problem?"

"Yes, of course."

She waited for him to say something about how much he'd appreciated her effort over the years, and how the family would miss her, but no. "Just send a text when it's arranged."

She called Alyssa, who whooped and said yes without a second's pause for thought. On Tuesday, Lee saw snow-sports school director Chris Logan in his office and handed in her resignation, effective at the end of the coming weekend, which she knew would be a busy one.

"If it's too soon, Chris, I can hold off another couple of weeks," she offered, "but I'd rather not, as long as it doesn't cause you problems. I'm planning to move back east and my baby sister is getting married the weekend after next. If I can finish Sunday, then I can start the drive Monday and be home in time for the wedding, instead of flying back and forth."

"Right." He nodded. "You put in for leave for the wedding weeks ago, I remember."

"I did, but there's been a change of plan, and it's likely that I'm making a permanent move."

"Not a problem at this end?"

"No." She had her story ready. "My parents have retired and my sisters have taken over running the family business, a vacation resort, and it's having a major remodel. They could do with some help, it turns out."

I'll be needing family help of a different kind....

He nodded and didn't push for more detail. "It's fine. Do it the way you want. Go sooner, even. It's a big drive. If you want to get there in time to help with the wedding preparations, or whatever. We have part-timers keen to move up to full time. A couple of them would probably help you pack, if it meant getting your job from you faster."

"Thanks." She wasn't surprised at this. She knew the drill with young instructors hungry for more work. "You mean it about going earlier?"

"If you want. The junior coaching program is in good hands with Everard. We'll be sorry to lose you, very sorry, but your plan makes sense."

"Thanks," she repeated. "I'll miss—well, I'll miss an awful lot." And yet in the back of her mind there was the realization that she wasn't leaving much of a mark. A handful of people would miss her, but the roots she'd put down here didn't go very deep.

"You must be pretty fond of your sisters," Chris was saying.

She nodded and smiled, and all the things she wasn't saying out loud bubbled inside her, ready to be said tonight to Mac.

Mac, who really shouldn't be the last to know, but somehow it had worked out that way.

"Let's go out," he said to her after they'd both wound up for the day.

"Out? Really?"

"Haven't seen you. Want some quality time."

"We usually do our quality time in a horizontal position."

"We can get to that later. And we will…." He smiled and reached to touch her, but she stepped away, as if she hadn't noticed. She couldn't kiss him and pretend there was nothing on her mind. The burden of her secret grew heavier every hour, and the uncertainty was making her jittery and miserable.

Should she have forced the conversation sooner? Should she have held off on any action until they'd talked?

But even without touching him, she wasn't hiding her reluctance well enough. He went on, "C'mon. I thought we could make it a little fancier than usual, but if you don't want that, then we'll sit in a booth at Waterstreet like always. I feel like steak. We can head there right now, have a beer and a meal, be home by seven-thirty."

"We could," she agreed. Where did you go to have a major conversation such as this one? Surely not to a bar? Now that she'd thoroughly made up her mind to tell him tonight, and had run out of good excuses—wasn't even looking for them anymore—she wanted to bite the bullet.

"What's our alternative?" he said. "Those people still invading our space?" He meant the friends of the Narmans.

He had a point. "They were leaving today, but I don't know what time," she said.

After a day of teaching on a freezing mountain, cereal and cold milk didn't cut it for an evening meal. They'd been stopping in at the bar for a hearty feed quite often over the past couple months. Everyone knew they were together, because they hadn't made any attempt at secrecy. When Lee's friends asked if it was serious, she only shrugged and answered, "Don't know. Don't think so. But it's fun." She didn't know what Mac said to his friends, or if they even asked.

"You're no fun tonight," he told her, softening the words by pulling her against him and planting a couple of crooked kisses somewhere in the region of her mouth. This time she couldn't help kissing him back. He tasted perfect, like always.

"Sorry," she said, and steak did sound good. With a heap of sides and possibly dessert. One thing she most definitely wasn't having so far, despite all the clichés about early pregnancy, was morning sickness. She felt as hungry as a horse and was sleeping like the dead, most nights. "We'll go to Waterstreet."

Seated in a booth just ten minutes later, they ordered sodas to start, each gulping half a glass of cold, sweet liquid without pausing for breath. Lee decided on prime rib, baked potato and salad, with a cup of clam chowder to start, and the soup arrived within a minute or two of their drinks. Mac was eating wings before his steak. "Man, I'm so hungry!"

"Me, too."

"Have some of the wings."

"No, the soup is really good. I'll stick to that."

Their steaks arrived as promptly as their appetizers and sodas. Mac had finished his drink, and ordered two beers—their usual kind—without consulting Lee. Gulping a mouthful of soup, she added quickly to the waitress, "And a soda water," before the girl hurried off again.

He looked a little surprised and Lee said, "Thirsty," because she could see a couple of friends about to come past, looking as if they were going to stop and say hello. They'd gone again by the time the beers and soda water arrived.

Mac pushed one of the beers in her direction, and she pushed it back to him, saying, "That's for you. I'm just having the soda water."

"Hey, I'm the one who should still be nursing my liver, not you."

"You won't have both of them?"

He shook his head. "They're way out of date, in Idaho, about how much I drink. One is plenty tonight."

"I should have changed the drink order then, not just added to it. I'm sorry."

"You don't have to keep apologizing."

"Sorry."

"Did it again."

"I know, I…" She took a deep breath. "Um, Mac?"

"What's up?"

"Something I have to tell you."

Instantly, a look of alarm appeared on his face. Every red-blooded male in America knew that when a woman spoke those words, the outcome wouldn't be good.

Just say it, Lee. Put both of us out of our misery.

"I did a pregnancy test while you were away."

He cursed under his breath. The alarmed expression

kicked up several notches. She didn't even need to say the word *positive*. It was obvious. He looked as stunned as she'd felt. "Damn, I don't believe this!" He looked like a single man in his thirties who had a great job offer waiting in the wings, who wasn't ready to settle down, and who suddenly saw suburbia staring at him out of his girlfriend's eyes.

Was that all it was?

All? It's enough, isn't it?

She thought she saw something else lurking in the depths of his eyes, or in the way his body had gone so still and tight, but she didn't know what it was, or if it was really even there. He muttered something. Curse words? She wasn't sure. The shock in his face didn't surprise her, but a feeling of aloneness and disappointment stirred within her. Maybe, irrationally, she'd craved something different.

Like what? She didn't even know.

"I'm...sorry, Mac."

"Will you stop that?" he hissed at her.

What had she expected? What had she *wanted*? He was no more shocked, and no more ready for this, than she was. It had hit both of them like a bolt from the blue, only the bolts had come several days apart.

Someone else was coming over to their booth, an instructor named Adam who embodied all Lee's reasons for avoiding short-term flings with young, athletic, hard-living males.

Is Mac one of those? Is that what his reaction's about?

"I've had some time to think," she told him quickly.

"I haven't. I can't believe this...."

"I know, which is why you can relax and stop looking like that, because I've thought it all through."

"Yeah?" He almost looked as if he was about to laugh, but cynically or even bitterly, not because this was in any way funny.

"This is not going to wreck your life," she said.

"Mac, my man! How's it hangin'?"

"Good, Adam, great." He and Adam did a bit of arm-punching and fist-bumping, with such an exaggerated attitude of male bonding that Lee knew on Mac's part it couldn't possibly be sincere. "Listen, bud, we're in the middle of something," he quickly said.

"No problem. Catch you later. We're over there."

"Right. Great… Let's get out of here," he muttered to Lee as soon as Adam had gone. "We can't— We need air. Or no interruptions. I'm not doing it like this. It's too— Let's just go." He stood up, flung some bills on the table to settle the tab and watched as she stood up, too. Neither of them had quite finished, but her appetite had vanished, and she thought his probably had, just as thoroughly.

Out in the snow, she asked him, "Where do you want to go?"

"Your place. I'm not talking about this in the middle of the street." But he did, adding after half a minute of silence, "Did you suspect? I mean, you did a test. While I was away. Without a word before that. Were you…? I mean, I presume you were late or something. Having symptoms. Nausea and sore breasts. Did you wait for me to go to Idaho, so that you could do it in secret?"

"No." She swore mildly, but with force. "I haven't had a lot of symptoms yet, and I haven't tried to hide anything, Mac."

She was shocked that he seemed angry about this, as if it was all her fault. As if the word *fault* was even relevant. She didn't think it was, and she'd never thought of him as the kind of man who might cast blame.

"It didn't occur to me I could be pregnant until a few days ago, after you'd already left," she said. "There was all that travel. I lost track of dates. I'm not feeling sick or anything. Tired, I guess. But then I work hard. And we don't sleep enough." She gave him a sideways glance, but he ignored the innuendo.

"How far along are you?"

"I don't know. A few weeks. You're right, my breasts are a little sore."

"A few weeks? No one's a few weeks. They count it from your last period. So when was that?"

She couldn't tell him. Mid-January? It had been pretty light.

"A doctor's going to want to know, to work out your due date."

"Well, it's going to have to be a rough estimate," she retorted, because the thing about the doctor sounded like an accusation.

"You should cut back on classes," Mac said. "You should talk to Chris."

"I have talked to Chris, and—"

"Good. One thing we agree on."

"What don't we agree on?"

Another short silence. "Let's not talk yet."

"You said that before, and then you started hitting me with questions."

"Okay, no more questions till we're home." He used the word casually, but it was wrong. They weren't living together. They'd never talked about it. Well...*never*? Never wasn't a long time, in this case. They'd known each other less than three months.

After a few minutes they came in sight of the Narman residence, which Lee was glad to find largely in darkness. The weekend visitors had left.

The visitors had left a door open. She saw a length of drape billowing through one of the French doors that led to the big deck that overlooked the slopes, and told Mac, "We're going to have to check the house. They haven't closed it up properly. Or else someone's broken in. They can't have set the alarm or it'd have gone off, with that door left open."

"Now?"

"Yes. I really can't leave it."

"I guess not. It's pretty obvious with that fabric blowing through. Anyone could have seen it."

"I hope nobody has."

As she unlocked the main door, he stood beside her, moving restlessly as if impatient to get this started. Inside, it was quickly apparent that the visitors hadn't cleaned up. There were empty take-out containers and pizza boxes strewn through the rooms, as well as dirty crockery and glassware, trails of crumbs and candy wrappers, wet towels on bathroom floors, sticky spills in the kitchen that hadn't been mopped up.

"Leave it," Mac told her, as she walked around, assessing the damage and the work.

"I don't think anything's actually broken or stained," she said. "And there's no sign of a break-in." She went over to the open door, pulled the billowing drape back inside, and closed and locked it. "It's freezing in here, even with the heating on. That door's been open for hours."

"Leave it. We're trying to talk about something important, and you're thinking about stains and security. Enough interruptions."

"I'm sorry."

His voice gentled. "And enough damned apologies!"

"Yeah, okay, I don't know why I keep doing that."

"You said you've decided what you're going to do." The words he'd chosen seemed to distance him from the whole issue. From the idea of a baby. From any thought of a new kind of link between them. There was a hardness to them and a woodenness that she couldn't read, but it seemed likely that she'd been right to think he wouldn't want to be involved.

She took her cue from his attitude and made her voice cool and firm. "I'm going back east." Because, really, what was the alternative? Stay here to create some messy arrangement of custody and access to a child who was still seven months away from being born? When she and Mac had said nothing, ever, about a future together? "To my family. Aspen isn't a town where I'd want to be bringing up a child on my own."

He didn't say a word. She looked at him and his face was like granite. She couldn't read it at all. He reached out and picked up a pizza box from a side table, and then another one from the arm of a couch. So they were cleaning up, after all? She was just about to start on it, too, when he asked neutrally, "So when are you planning to leave?"

"As soon as I'm ready."

"What, tonight?" It was sarcastic and steely.

"No, not tonight. Of course not tonight, Mac! Do we need to make this hostile? If you want something different, then spell it out!"

"Spell it out?" he muttered. "Hell!"

"Yes," she agreed, although she didn't know quite what she was agreeing to. That this was difficult and not fun. That when it came to serious stuff, they had nothing to draw on, no blueprint, no rules.

"So, when?"

"Maybe Friday." She'd been thinking about it since Chris had given her the go-ahead to be flexible, and figured Friday was the best she could manage. Now that she was leaving, now that she'd realized what a small dent she'd made in this place and how few ties she had, she was impatient about it.

She kept thinking about Daisy and Mary Jane and how great it would be to have them in her life again, not just occasionally at Thanksgiving or Christmas, if she went for a visit or if they came here, but day to day.

Grabbing a coffee together.

Watching the same TV shows, in the same time zone.

Yelling at each other over some sister thing, then laughing with their next breath.

Daisy and Tucker were about to get married. Maybe there'd soon be a tiny cousin for this baby inside her, who wasn't yet real. Wouldn't that be great?

The ties of family were tugging on Lee in a way they hadn't tugged in years.

"Friday," Mac echoed. He muttered half to himself, "That's probably when I'll hear about the job...."

"If I can get everything done by then."

"This isn't happening." He seemed lost, standing there with the pizza boxes in his hands. His whole being seemed focused on some private darkness that she didn't understand. "This just is not happening."

"Well, it is." She gently took them from him, added another one to the pile and he didn't protest. "Are you saying I should be handling it differently?"

"I don't know what I'm saying. I'm not saying anything. I'm telling you to take it seriously."

"I am. We've known each other eleven weeks, Mac."

"Yeah. I know. Yeah." He focused on her movement. "You really are going to clean up?"

"You were the one who started picking up boxes. And it's Tuesday night. I have a lot to do in two days."

"I guess you do."

"I'm sorry."

This time, he didn't object to the apology. "If you don't mind," he said, "I won't stay to help. I just need some time."

Chapter Seven

Upstate New York, April

"We never ended it," Mac said.

"I left and you didn't stop me. We never said anything about it not ending." Lee hugged her robe tighter around her, wishing she was dressed. It was ten-thirty in the morning. Wearing a robe at this hour had stopped feeling comforting and pretty sexy with Mac around, the way it had felt at first. Now it felt frumpish and lazy, and it put her at a disadvantage when he looked so good and so relaxed in his shirt and jeans. "We said goodbye."

Goodbye had been pretty horrible, in fact. They hadn't had a private moment together after he left the messy Narman residence that Tuesday night. She'd been so busy packing her possessions, in between teaching a reduced load of classes on the slopes, deciding which things to ship east, which to take with her when she drove, and which to give away or throw away or sell.

Her mugs, what should she do with her mugs? In the end, she'd packed them all in bubble wrap, put them in boxes and brought them with her, on the backseat of her car. The mugs weren't important. She had no idea what was important right now.

She'd avoided Mac and he must have been avoiding her, she thought, because it was almost spooky the way their paths failed to cross. Then on Thursday evening, when everything was done and Alyssa had already moved into the janitor's apartment—Lee planned to spend her last night in Aspen in one of the Narman bedrooms upstairs—she went to the ski school office to collect some final paperwork and say some goodbyes, and there he was.

It seemed as good a time as any. What were they supposed to do? Create a special occasion for it? That would be more horrible than anything.

So they'd said goodbye in front of about six other people, with one short kiss and a superficial few words. It was so easy to keep in touch, now, with texts and calls and email and Skype, and neither of them said a word about whether they would. He still seemed to be in shock, and suffering through a whole lot of issues he clearly wasn't planning to share with her.

She'd left early Friday morning, and had spun the drive out over five days, because the tiredness increased daily, and the morning sickness kicked in, exacerbated by the fatigue and by the junk food options available en route. She found she had to make proper rest stops and go to proper stores and find fruit and decent bread and fresh juice and salad sandwiches, because burgers and fries and soda were too horrible to contemplate.

She'd arrived at Spruce Bay on Tuesday afternoon, six days ago, to find Daisy as serene and fresh and cheerful as her namesake flower about the coming wedding. Any residual awkwardness over the fact that her fiancé, Tucker Reid, had once been planning to marry Lee herself was quickly smoothed over.

That was more than ten years ago. It had never been the right plan. From the beginning it had happened for the wrong reasons. Now, Tucker was visibly in thrall of

Daisy's bright, creative and very feminine energy, and Lee just wasn't that kind of girl. If there was anyone she was aching for, it was Mac, and that didn't make any sense, because they'd never said they loved each other. They'd never thought about it. They'd just taken the whole thing day to day.

Watching Daisy and Tucker during their simple wedding ceremony, with the bride looking so beautiful in a floaty dress with sheer, tiny sleeves, and the groom totally unable to hide his love and desire, Lee had tried to put herself and Mac in their place, there at the altar, and couldn't picture it.

He hadn't been in touch. He might be packing up to move back to Idaho. He would surely have heard about the job at Barrier Mountain by now. What had they ever had together that could make her believe in this kind of a future? Flowers and a veil and the promise of undying love… No. They hadn't been heading in that direction at all. They'd said nothing to each other about anything like that.

"But we never actually ended it," he repeated now.

"No, we didn't."

"And if you hadn't gotten pregnant, what would have happened? Were you planning to end it, before that happened?"

"Not at that point. I—"

"Not at that point?"

"We met at a bar in a resort town, Mac. In that situation, you're not looking for something long-term, and you kind of assume the other person isn't, either."

"Right." After a moment, he added quietly, "Are you really that cynical and hard-edged? You were that ready to dump the whole thing the moment it threatened to go deeper?"

"No! I was…really enjoying it, if you want the truth. Every bit of it."

Scaring myself a little, wondering once or twice if I was being played.

"So why end it just because something changed?"

"A pretty big thing changed," she pointed out.

"Yes. Something we should have talked about, and thought about, and made decisions about together. Something really—" he took a breath "—confronting."

"Confronting?"

"Yes! For me. Can't speak for you. And you presented me with a done deal, at a point where I had decisions to make about my own future, and then before I could think anything through, you'd just gone."

"Are you saying you were looking to settle down? Are you saying you *weren't* living the stereotypical ski bum bachelor lifestyle?"

He flinched visibly, but his reply was a casual drawl, with a crooked smile. "Ski bum is a little harsh. You'd have to go to Adam Panik for that."

She ignored him, since she couldn't tell if he was seriously upset about the accusation, or what. "Are you saying you'd given me any signal or indication whatsoever that you were looking for something more than a seasonal fling? Not even a full season! You were talking about moving back to Idaho. You were excited about it. You said you hadn't made up your mind, but everything in the way you talked about the job said that you wanted to take it. You'd had a really good time partying with your friends and family, and you were looking forward to more of that, too. What happened, by the way? Did you get the job?"

"Yes, I got it. They called Friday afternoon, would

have been about five hours after you left. They wanted me to go back up to talk through a few final details."

"So why aren't you there?"

"I wanted to take it. But I turned it down."

"Why? If you wanted it?"

"Hell, Lee!" He pivoted on his heels and slammed a fist on the counter. "To come east. To be a father."

"Just like that."

"No, not just like that. Didn't you leave Aspen and come here just like that?"

"I have family here."

"So do I. I have a child."

"Not yet."

"Yes, yet." He closed the space between them and laid his hand on her stomach, through the bunched thickness of the robe. The mix of possession and nurturing in his touch robbed her of breath, and she could feel his aura around her like something warm and heavy and good. "I have a child. Here. Inside you. Real and alive and needing me for protection. What else was I going to do?"

Her heart lurched. It was such a huge statement about his intention to stay involved that she didn't know what to do, how to feel. This wash of relief, for example, was it pure illusion? What did she want from him? He'd spoken with more anger than love, and she didn't know what to think about that.

He slid his other arm around her shoulder so that she was cradled in his embrace, feeling the wall of his chest behind her. She wanted to lean back against him, turn her cheek to pillow it against his shirt. But if she did that, if she accepted this, wasn't she just ignoring all the things they hadn't yet resolved?

His palm rested below her navel, where you couldn't feel the baby yet, even though her stomach was so taut and flat. Those muscles would be softening soon, to allow her body to stretch and expand, but it hadn't happened so far. "Can you feel it?" he asked, as if his thoughts had run in the same direction.

"Not yet."

"Have you seen a doctor?"

"I have an appointment for tomorrow."

"So I arrived on the right day."

She pushed herself out of his arms and pivoted to face him. "You're acting as if this is simple, and it's not."

"It is for me. Well, some of it."

"It isn't. It can't be."

"The welfare of the baby—that's simple." His dark eyes glittered. "It's my baby, too, and you're not going to shut me out. You're not going to make decisions that I don't have a say in. And you're not going to keep on living your life as if nothing's happened. I'm here to make sure of that."

He sounded so strong and forceful about it that he almost scared her. Angered her, too. "There's no need for you to act like we're in a battle over that, Mac. What gives you any reason to think I'm going to live my life as if nothing's happened? I know something has, and I'm taking it seriously, and I don't see why you would assume any different."

"Maybe not," he growled. "That's yet to be seen."

She had to fight herself back to a place where she could talk in rational words. She took a deep breath. "There are two separate things going on here. There's the fact that we're having a baby together, and there's the question of whether we have a relationship, and I'm not going to mix those up."

"Aren't they mixed up already?"

"No! I'm not going to make the massive mistake of thinking that your being involved with the pregnancy and the baby means you and I are together. That would be all wrong. You cannot stay here in the apartment, Mac! You cannot barge in here and demand accommodation, when we don't know if we even have a relationship."

"Of course not." He swore under his breath and began pacing the kitchen again.

He'd brought her up short. "But you said—"

"You really don't think very highly of me, do you?"

"Mac—"

"As anything other than a bed partner, that is."

"You said—"

"I wasn't serious. Do you honestly think I'm going to forcibly camp out here until we've agreed on a custody arrangement?"

"No, I—"

He looked at her. "Oh, wait a minute, no! You thought I was going to muscle in here and court you until you swore undying love."

"I don't know what I thought," she said flatly, because he made it all sound ridiculous. "You were the one who said it."

"I wasn't serious," he repeated. "I was making a point."

"What point?"

"That I'm here. That I'm a part of this."

"So where will you go? How will you manage? What will you do?"

"You really, really do not think highly of me."

If he'd been angry when he first showed up, he was angrier now.

White with it.

Eyes narrowed and still glittering.

Mouth hard.

There was no question of softening him with a kiss, reminding him what they'd had together in Colorado. They were way beyond that. She felt deeply in the wrong, and yet incapable of apology because she didn't understand where he was coming from.

"Believe it or not, I'm not broke, Lee."

"I never said—"

"I have savings. I have a good résumé. And as my mom has said to me about a thousand times, I don't have a lazy bone in my body. I wasn't planning to scrounge off you while I sat and watched TV all day."

"Mac, I never said—"

"I'll find accommodation, I'll check out the whole area and I'll start looking for a job. The people at Barrier Mountain were pretty flattering in how keen they were to have me. I'm thinking it shouldn't be too hard to find something here."

"No, that's true."

"And it seems like you were right. We did end it in Colorado. The relationship, that is. The involvement, no. Because I'm not going to father a child that disappears from my life." His voice cracked. "I'm not going to let you handle the pregnancy without my input. And I'm not going to stay conveniently two thousand miles away so that you don't have to deal with me. I don't know what I ever said or did to make you think that was what I'd want."

He was right. On this point, he was completely right, and she felt ill about it, and deeply ashamed. "I shouldn't have made assumptions."

"No. You shouldn't. You should have given me time. I'm going to skip the coffee." He went to the door and was already at the top of the stairs when he turned and told her, "Text me the time and address for the appointment tomorrow, and the name of the doctor. I'll see you there."

Chapter Eight

He was already waiting when she arrived at the obstetrician's office the next morning, shortly before the scheduled appointment time, his hands pushed into the pockets of his jacket and his shoulders hunched.

The ob-gyn group practice was housed in a beautifully restored Victorian in the nearby town of Odinville, with turrets and bay windows and wraparound verandas, surrounded by garden. Lee thought it would be a beautiful place to come to for her prenatal appointments, watching the spring and summer unfold as her body changed and the baby grew.

Mac looked very different, pacing up and down in front of the building, to the way he'd looked yesterday. He'd shaved and slept, and the red-eyed and rumpled look that came from two thousand miles of driving had disappeared. As well, she realized, he'd dressed for this.

She'd never seen these clothes before—a charcoal-gray suede jacket, a classic pair of dark pants with a button-down shirt in a subtle, textured pattern of blues and grays, black shoes that could have worked for office or hiking or bar. She'd seen him only in ski pants and jacket and boots, or jeans and T-shirt and running shoes.

He'd dressed for the doctor, she realized, dressed to prove something about his worth and his intentions as a father-to-be. She couldn't easily have shut him out of this, even if she'd wanted to.

And she didn't want to, she knew.

In that area, there was a lot still to explore, but there was a huge part of her that was so, so happy that he'd shown up here, despite yesterday's anger on both sides.

Speaking of that…

"Ah, look…I came on too strong yesterday," he told her, as soon as they'd said hello. The words came rushing out as if he'd had them ready for hours.

"Yeah?" she said. Was it an apology? For which particular bit?

"I was tired. And angry," he added after a stretched-out beat of silence. "And scared."

"Scared, Mac?" The sky was gray today, and there was a chilly wind blowing. He hadn't needed to wait out here in the cold for her. "Scared of what?"

"Well, first, that you may have put two thousand miles between us because you really, by hook or by crook, weren't going to let me be involved."

"Only because I thought you didn't want to be, and I didn't want to be stuck in Aspen raising a child on my own, passing my child's father in the street and watching you not even acknowledge your—" She stopped, seeing his anger rise again, and held up her hand to ward off another round of harsh words. "Yes, I know I shouldn't have assumed you would act like that, but…I guess I was scared, too. This is new and unexpected and off track for me, too."

Her voice had gone husky. He heard it and looked at her with an extra layer of curiosity added to what was already a complicated mix of feeling. "Off track?" His eyes had narrowed.

"I hadn't thought about parenthood. I was happy. I had my life set up exactly the way I wanted."

"You didn't want to be a mother?" There was something in his expression that she didn't understand, but since they seemed to be trying to meet each other halfway today, she let it go.

"I'd thought that I might want to," she said, trying for full honesty. "Someday. In my head it was still at least two or three years in the future, with a lot of emotional mileage to travel, as well as time. I thought I would need to talk about it and think about it long and hard, with the right person, after the two of us had spent a long time and a lot of thought working out whether he *was* the right person—"

"You mean this faceless man who might be the father, if you both decided you wanted to?"

"Yes. I always thought it would be really important to be sure I was taking a huge step like that for the right reasons."

"And instead it's come at you out of the blue, and instead of some perfect man in a long-term relationship, you're stuck with me. After twelve weeks." He pushed his hands deeper into the pockets of his jacket.

"No, that's not what I meant. We've got each other. You're as much stuck with me as a mother as I'm stuck with you. And I—I'm really sorry about handling this so badly."

"Stuck with my DNA, my income, my bizarre ideas on how to raise a kid…"

He wanted her to laugh at that, but she couldn't. Not quite. Not yet. Maybe he did have bizarre ideas. Maybe *she* did. "We haven't thought long and hard about very much, Mac."

"Yet."

"Yet. I mean, for all I know you could have a child already."

There was a beat of silence. "I don't," he said. Then he repeated it. "I don't." He shot her a look. "Would it be a problem if I did?"

"Well, I'd want to conduct an extensive interview with the mother."

Lee waited for him to laugh, or at least smile, but he didn't. He was frowning and staring into the distance, and there was something going on here that she didn't understand. He'd said he didn't have a child. Said it bluntly with no room for doubt, and yet there'd been a hesitation. All of a sudden, she wondered whether she believed him. Would he really lie to her about something like that?

"Why are we standing here?" he asked abruptly.

"Because you served up a deep and meaningful discussion before we'd even made it inside."

"We had to, didn't we?"

"Yes, but the timing and the location aren't ideal."

"No. True."

"Are we done? Is there anything else you wanted to tell me?" There was. She could feel it.

But he shook his head. "What's the time?" He pulled his phone from his pocket and answered his own question. "We're due. Better go in. They probably have a heap of stuff for us to fill in."

"Where did you stay last night?" she blurted out as they climbed the wooden steps to the veranda. She felt like a jealous wife questioning her husband's movements.

"I found a place that had vacation housekeeping cottages, just a minute or so from exit 21 on I-87. Took one on a week-by-week arrangement. I don't want to take a lease on a place yet. If I end up working farther north, at Whiteface or Titus Mountain or somewhere, I'd be looking for something in that direction."

"Right. I suppose that makes sense." Whiteface was nearly two hours' drive, Titus, even farther. Accommodation near the snowfields was expensive, but you could find something affordable if you were prepared to live on one of the back roads.

He opened the door for her, and she was still thinking about his plans, the way they seemed so independent of her own. He might be living two hours away, this time next week. And yet when it came to the pregnancy and the baby, he had no hesitation about saying he wanted to stay close and fully involved.

"What are we going to say about our relationship?" she asked Mac quietly, when they were seated and she was filling in the forms he'd correctly predicted.

"Not their business, is it?"

"But it's going to come up. Dr. Cartwright is going to have to call us each something. 'Your wife.' 'Your partner.' Unless she's one of those people who refer to all pregnant women as Mom."

"Then let her call me 'your partner' or 'Dad,' I don't care."

I care.

It bothered her that they might both get trapped in a role that didn't fit and wasn't true. Husband and wife, or even amicable exes. She didn't know what they were, or what they were going to be.

Not together. That seemed to be clear.

But so closely linked.

It was weird. Uncomfortable. Not fun.

She kept trying to forget about his body, about the

easy way she'd claimed it in Colorado, and enjoyed it, and felt so easy with him on so many levels.

Casual levels.

Nothing was casual anymore. She was still so aware of him, every minute they were in the same space. Filling in her forms, she felt every movement he made—the crossing and uncrossing of his legs, the sigh of boredom, the way he ran his hand over his jaw. He couldn't find a magazine that appealed, and the TV in the waiting room was tuned to a local morning talk show where the hosts were currently enthusing about some amazing new kind of therapy, involving salt or seaweed or something.

Lee wanted to lean into Mac and tell him to chill, give him a saucy kiss with a promise in it for later, ask about lunch, the way she would have before.

The way they were both so *good* at, before.

There seemed to be this huge dividing line between Before Pregnancy Test and After Pregnancy Test, and she didn't know how to behave in this new universe, the way she'd never known how to be a proper bride-to-be ten years ago with Tucker.

It wasn't just Mac's fault. She knew that. Maybe it wasn't his fault at all. Maybe it was all her. She was a cat, and she wanted to walk alone. Was that it? When it was time to give birth, who knew, she'd probably slink off somewhere and have her kitten on a pile of newspaper in the bottom of a broom closet.

Could she share this joke with him? Would he laugh?

Somehow she thought not. She had a gut sense that in some way it would cut too close to the bone.

Anyhow, it was too late. "Lee Cherry?" said one of the nurses. Time to go in.

* * *

"That went okay," Mac said. Once more they were standing in front of the old Victorian that housed the ob-gyn practice, not ready to part company just yet.

She could feel the relief in him. He seemed giddy about it, as if he'd feared something very different, and, okay, she felt the same, so she shouldn't question the undercurrents she could detect in him. She agreed with a smile. "Yes, it was good."

Better than good.

They had a due date, September 23, and a theory about those condoms in her drawer. They'd been just a little too close to their use-by date, and the period she'd vaguely remembered from January hadn't been a period at all. Apparently women quite often had some light bleeding in early pregnancy, so it had been an easy mistake to make, and Lee was already close to the three-month mark.

"Feels like coming out of the principal's office after not getting detention," Mac said.

"Oh, that happened a lot to you?"

"Detention, hell, yeah. Getting out of it, not so much."

"What did you do, in high school?"

"Few things. Nothing really bad. The police were never called in."

"Good to know. What was the worst?"

"Setting fire to the girls' locker room."

"And the police weren't called for that?"

"It was an accident!" he protested, with wounded puppy eyes.

"I'm not going to ask."

They grinned at each other, happy about the easy back and forth between them. It was familiar and good and a relief. The grins stayed, turning into smiles that were soft at the edges, and a long, long sizzling look. He was such a beautiful man. She loved the shape of him, the taste of him, the soul in his eyes. Her heart flipped. She didn't want the distance between them. She didn't want to forget the fun they had together when they talked.

Didn't seem as if he wanted to forget it, either, because the look between them held and held, and his shoulders relaxed, and when she stepped a little closer, without even knowing her feet were going to move, he didn't step away. He held out his hands and she took them and they both squeezed, letting their fingers tangle and caress. Then he bent and kissed her, just one swift, soft touch across her mouth that was gone before she could kiss him back.

"I'm not nearly so much of a bad boy now, I promise," he said.

"You can be a little bad, if you want...."

"Yeah?"

"Like me a bad boy, I do."

It was the best moment they'd had since she'd told him she was pregnant. This was how it used to be, in Colorado. If they could just get back to that...

"Want to go for coffee?" he asked.

"I wish I could, but there's a delivery coming this afternoon, and I need to be there for it."

The appointment had taken longer than she'd expected. She'd thought they would be in and out in twenty minutes, a piece of naiveté on her part that she didn't want him to guess, since in fact they'd been there well over an hour, and busy for all of it, seeing the nurse, the obstetrician and the office manager. Mac hadn't seemed surprised about all the questions and the big dump of information. His sister had kids, Lee knew. He'd apparently picked up a few things.

The truth was, she didn't know a whole lot about pregnancy, herself. She wasn't one of those people who'd been able to calculate her due date before she even got to the doctor's office, and who knew about five different pregnancy books off by heart. She didn't even have a pregnancy book yet.

Must get one.

"Coffee at your place, then," he suggested.

"It's out of your way."

"I have nothing major scheduled for today, maybe a couple of phone calls is all, so that's not a problem."

"Okay, then. Coffee would be good."

They both hesitated. She wanted to touch him, disappear into his arms, but that didn't work anymore. It wasn't part of the agreement. They didn't really have an agreement, just a rather angry decision yesterday that they weren't together now as a couple, and it felt weird. She didn't feel as if they weren't together.

"Hey…seeing the heartbeat was great, wasn't it?" he said. "Really good."

"I know! I had no idea we would. That we could. Already."

"Didn't you?"

"No! When she put the wand thing on my stomach I couldn't work out what we were seeing at all, but then when she got to the heart and there it was, pumping away, and we could see the rhythm and the movement…wow!"

"I know. It was amazing." He smiled, and that seemed to give them both a way to turn their backs on each other and head to their cars. "See you back at the ranch."

"Yep. Half an hour."

She liked him.

She really, really liked him.

If I wasn't having this baby, we could have just kept going with no pressure. We wouldn't have needed any decisions or plans or compromises or labels. We wouldn't have had to wonder about what we felt or why we were together. Those are the things that are giving us trouble.

For a moment, she felt an intense flood of irritation and anger and regret at the way the positive pregnancy test had mucked up her life, and maybe some anger at herself, too, for not being the kind of person who could just go off to a clinic and get rid of it. But then she stopped short, appalled by the coldness of some of those phrases.

Mucked up my life... Get rid of it.

No.

No, never!

There was a beating heart inside her.

There was a tiny little being, gender as yet unknown, beavering away the best it knew how, growing and developing and becoming a person, working for life, depending on her, surviving on the nourishment from her body, utterly vulnerable to every choice she made, every morsel she ate, every mouthful she drank, taking its first tenacious steps along its path to the future.

Mucking up her life?

No!

Dear Lord, dear baby, darling baby, I don't feel that way. I couldn't. I never will again. I'll make this work, I promise you. I love you.

She blinked back tears of intensely powerful emotion, and had to take the slow lane on the highway until she was sure she could see well enough to keep going. She knew that whatever happened from now on, she would never wish the baby away. She had a need to love and cherish this little being, a need she'd never known before, and it was good…wonderful…better than she'd ever imagined.

Mac was already waiting for her in a parking space outside the Spruce Bay Resort office. The landscaping crew from Tucker's company had been here this morning, preparing the beds for the spring planting that would soon take place, but they'd left now, and as yet there was no sign of the truck that was supposed to be bringing supplies of wine, beer and spirits for the restaurant bar.

They went inside and up the stairs, and Mac followed her the way he had yesterday. Except he was closer, she was sure of it. Wasn't that the warmth of him she could feel? And the eddies of air created by his movement? He'd lost all of yesterday's bristling anger.

Coffee together in the Cherry family kitchen felt like a do-over, a chance to get it right this time. Yesterday, she'd made some but they never drank it, never even took out the mugs.

"You've unpacked your mugs," he noticed now.

"Yep, but Mary Jane's made me put half of them back in a box because there isn't room."

"You have the book cover mugs out of the box. Does the same rule still apply as before?"

"Oh, absolutely."

"Good, because I've added another one to the list."

She laughed. "You're crazy."

"Hey, I have my eReader—the world of books is my intellectual oyster. Your mugs are as good a guide as any to what I should download next."

"So which new one are you allowed to drink from now?"

"*The Body in the Library.* Classic whodunit from the queen of crime."

"You're picking all the short, easy books. That's possibly cheating. I'll have to consult the rule book."

"Fine, I'll read *Great Expectations* next, if you want. Plus, I have to point out, *A Room of One's Own* wasn't exactly light, escapist reading, even if it was short."

"You really are crazy."

"You like that about me."

"I do."

They forgot that they weren't together anymore. It just felt so natural to move close and lean against each other and look into each other's eyes. He pressed his forehead against hers and brushed a kiss on her mouth, as soft as the one outside the doctor's, but longer.

"Promise me…" he whispered.

"Promise you what?" She touched his face, rediscovering the texture of his skin, the shape of him, the rightness of him.

He kissed away her smile, parting her lips with his, talking against her mouth. "That you'll take care of yourself. That you'll let me take care of you a little bit, too."

"I shouldn't like the sound of that so much."

And I shouldn't love the feel of my hands running over your backside so much, because it's distracting me.

"Why shouldn't you?" he murmured.

"Because I'm a cat, remember? I'm independent." She rubbed her cheek against his, and he turned into the contact and gave her a slow yet careless smooch.

"Cats love to be pampered," he said.

"Only on their own terms."

"What are your terms?"

"My terms, wow, I could get a really good deal out of this...."

"Seriously, Lee." He pulled back a little and looked at her, searching her face.

"Seriously, what? My terms?"

"Seriously promise you'll take care of yourself. And the baby. The absolute best you know how."

"Of course I will. You know I will." She touched his face again.

"Don't know it," he said in a mutter, "but if you're saying it, promising it..."

"I am, Mac. It was scary at first, yes, but now I believe in this baby with my whole heart. When I saw those tiny beats this morning..." Once more, she was blinking back tears.

"Then I believe you," he said slowly. But she wasn't sure that he did. He saw a tear brim over and slide down her cheek, and touched it with his fingertip, as if it was as precious as a diamond. He added in a different voice, just as complicated, "I do believe you. I have to, don't I? I have no choice."

He began to kiss her, at first as if searching for something, then fiercely and hungrily, on the corners of her mouth, in the middle, going deeper, and if kissing could create belief, then she was all for it. If kissing could *communicate* belief, then she was for it even more.

Yes, Mac, yes, I'll take care of myself. Why wouldn't I? Feel the way I'm holding you, feel the way I'm drinking the taste of you, and believe it.

She slid her hands up beneath his shirt to trace the shapes of the muscles in his back. She'd missed these. She'd missed all this. The distance between them those last few days in Colorado and then the long drive had made her forget, but now that he was here she remembered, and just needed it.

Needed him.

"You feel so good," he muttered.

"Can we go to bed?" she whispered into his mouth. "Please?"

He groaned and muttered, "How the hell do you think I'm going to say no to that?"

He scooped her into his arms and carried her like a bride across a threshold, as if she weighed about as much as the cat she might—not really—have been in a previous life. She rested her head against the hard pad of his shoulder muscle and let him do it. "Tell me which bedroom."

"Here."

"Single bed, Lee?" He looked down at her, black lashes almost sweeping against his cheeks, dark eyes glinting.

"We'll fit." That look had almost robbed her of breath.

"Stuff I might want to do to you that doesn't fit, quite…" He stood her on the floor and cupped his hand against the mound at the top of her thighs.

"So we'll squash in." Because she wasn't going to put a dampener on his intentions in that department.

"Are you always such an optimist?" He ran a finger along the seam of her jeans, the one that matched the seam in her body, where she was already swollen and moist.

"When it comes to sleeping with you," she answered shakily, "I've learned it pretty much always pays off."

"Let's just see then, shall we?" He unsnapped the jeans and slid them down, pulled off her top and bra, and kissed her across miles of skin, then knelt to bury his face in her lower belly and knead her backside with his gorgeous strong hands, while she ran her fingers through his hair.

I don't want to do it like this. Not again.

Mac shouldn't be thinking about it, not while he and Lee were making love—or she was trying to—but the gut-level resistance and reluctance wouldn't leave him on command. He loved her body, loved its sleek, toned muscle and the contrasting softness of her surprisingly full breasts and rounded butt. He loved the suppleness, and the rippling, and the depth of her breathing, and the ease in her when she stretched.

He'd always had a thing for women who managed to be superbly athletic yet very female at the same time, and it had cost him before. He'd gotten totally carried away by a beautiful, toned body and hadn't taken the slightest notice of anything else, until his casual attitude came back and bit him, and he probably still wasn't over what had happened after that.

He was over *her* totally, over Sloane.

But over *it,* no.

Hell, he didn't want to go there right now. He really didn't.

Lee's different, he told himself. *She's older. She's less driven. We have more together. We laugh more. She's kinder and more giving and—*

"Hey…" she whispered. "Are we on the same page, here?" She reached for him and pulled him farther up the bed so that they lay face-to-face. Her blue-green eyes dazzled him, and her soft mouth was flat and closed and serious, and he wanted to kiss it until it was panting and gasping and calling his name. "What's up, Mac?"

"Nothing. The doctor didn't say anything about this not being safe...."

"Which she would have, if it wasn't. I'm sure the whole world is full of pregnant people having sex. Personally, I'm liking it."

"Yeah?"

"I feel...squishier." She squirmed a little. "Rounder."

"Nothing round yet." He laid his hand on her stomach. He kept doing that, couldn't help himself. It was a promise, every time.

I'll protect you, baby. I'm here for you. You don't just have a mom, you have a dad, too, and this time I don't care what I have to do to keep you safe.

"Up here, I'm round," she said. "Feel. I have these lovely soft round melony balloony things." She took his hand and placed it on a breast, leaving him in no doubt about what he was supposed to do. And say.

"Wow, you do." He cupped each breast in turn, and felt how they'd grown. Her satiny skin was tight, and her hardened nipples practically jumped against his palm. They were darker, he realized. Bigger.

"And don't you like them?" she whispered.

"Have to admit...yeah. Very, very much." He leaned across and buried his face in the deepened cleft between them.

Man...

Then he sucked, cupping her gently, tracing the tip of his tongue around those darkened areolae and hearing her breathing quicken. Which made her breasts move up and down, tempting him to lick more and suck harder. Oh, wow. He felt the tightened creases beneath the new weight, and saw a faint, shadowy tracing of blue veins.

"And I like you liking them," she said, very unsteadily.

He teased her nipples with his knuckles, brushing them back and forth. She gasped and arched, and he rolled her on top of him so that the tight, hot globes grazed heavily against his chest. Then he took them in his hands again, the ridge of his erection pressing against her mound and her swollen lips.

Squishier, eh? Yes, he could feel. He pulled her against him and ran his hands over her butt. They fit so well. They just did. It was amazing.

"So let's get with the program, is what you're saying," he whispered.

"Is what I'm saying," she confirmed raggedly.

He got with the program.

Chapter Nine

"What are you listening for?" Mac asked Lee an hour or so later.

"The truck that's supposed to be bringing the liquor supplies. But that wasn't a truck I heard just now, it was a boat on the lake." They were still lying in her bed, replete and happy. Lee didn't dare talk too much just yet, in case she spoiled the mood.

This was all very tentative, what had just happened. She didn't know how to interpret it, how much to trust it. It seemed as if they were back to the way they'd been in Colorado, but she knew they weren't. They couldn't be. Too much had changed.

"When does your sister get back?" Mac asked.

"Which one?"

"The one who's getting back soon. The one who's living here. Mary Jane."

"Tomorrow."

"I don't think she's been gone nearly long enough."

"Oh, you don't?"

"Despite its inadequate size, I have to say this bed is more comfortable than the one in my cottage off of exit 21. And yet not quite as private as I'd like."

"Does that mean you're planning to be back in this bed again soon?" She couldn't quite hide that it was a loaded question.

And he was silent for a little too long. "I was angry yesterday," he said. He took a controlled breath. "And scared."

"Scared?"

"It's scary, having a baby. It's momentous. I reacted too strongly, and I shouldn't have. Maybe we should just coast for a while, see where this goes."

"It always seems to go to the same place."

"A pretty good place."

"No argument there." She snuggled against him, traced patterns with her fingers on his chest and ventured lower down.

"What did your family say about the baby?" he asked after a minute. "Are they okay with it?"

"I haven't told them."

As soon as she said it, she knew it would create a problem. She felt him stiffen. "You haven't told them," he repeated. He pushed her hand away, tilted his head and stared at her.

"Not yet. Early days, isn't it?"

His dark eyes narrowed. "So what do they think about you coming back here to live?"

I haven't told them that yet, either.

She didn't say it out loud, but her silence said it for her. When she'd arrived by car last week, four days before the wedding, instead of by airplane the day before, they'd all been surprised and a little concerned.

"I just needed a break," she'd told them. "Open-ended. Not sure what's happening."

Soon, she would have to ask about staying on here, whether there was an income for her in helping Mary Jane and Daisy run the resort, or whether she needed to work out something else. They should probably have a family meeting about it and formalize the decision.

Daisy had moved all her things to Tucker's very nice apartment above his landscaping business's office and showroom, but she would be running the Spruce Bay restaurant, open on a limited basis during their off-seasons and for three meals a day all summer, and so she would be here almost every day. Meanwhile, Mary Jane managed the accommodation side of the business, a role she'd gradually taken over from their parents the past few years. She made reservations, directed staff, troubleshooting the various problems that inevitably cropped up.

But with the renovation almost completed and the whole place looking better than it ever had, they would have increased occupancy rates and more work, and was that what Lee wanted? To help run the family business? Was she done with mountain guiding and ski instructing? Hard to combine those with pregnancy, but once the baby was born...?

"I don't want to tell them yet," she said firmly. "There's too much still undecided."

"By who? By us, do you mean?"

"Well, by me. First, anyhow, then..." She stopped.

He'd sat up and swiveled his body out of the narrow bed, the movement pulling on the sheet and dragging it down to her waist. Then he twisted around to look at her. "You are way too big on creating done deals without anyone else getting a say, do you know that?"

"Have *you* told people?" It was a rhetorical question, intended to silence him and put him on the back foot, but it failed completely.

"Yes, of course I have," he answered quietly. He twisted more, his naked side a smooth column of olive-skinned rib and muscle. "I've told my whole family. My parents, my sister and her husband, their kids."

"You called them before you left Colorado?" She bunched the sheet up to her neck. Whenever they made love, her body was so trusting—she never felt naked or vulnerable with him at all. She shivered with delight again now, just thinking about the way he'd touched and kissed her breasts, the way he'd moved inside her. But when they argued like this, everything was suddenly different. She needed the self-protection of a covering.

"No, I drove up there," he answered, "and we had a big talk about it. About what it meant. How I felt. How they felt. My sister's kids were thrilled at the idea of a baby cousin. For my parents it was…more complicated."

"You drove all the way to—? It has to be a fifteen-hour drive from Aspen to Coeur d'Alene!"

"Sixteen. Sixteen and a half, really." He'd withdrawn. She could feel it.

Well, she could see it. He was dressing with neat, staccato movements. Pulling on underwear, grabbing his shirt. Not looking at her now.

He was still talking in that quiet, dignified way that spooked her because it seemed to imply that in all sorts of emotional areas, she fell massively short. Was he right? He'd known in Colorado that she held herself back, that she liked her moments of independence, and it hadn't seemed to bother him.

"I wanted to tell them in person," he said. "Didn't seem like the kind of major life change to announce in a phone call."

"Sometimes it has to be." She was planning to call her own parents soon.

"Sometimes. Not this time. Not for me. It was only a week earlier that I'd been telling my mom I had no plans for a serious relationship or a family anytime soon. Yes, it's a sixteen-hour drive from Aspen to Coeur d'Alene, but it's almost a forty-hour drive from Coeur d'Alene to here. One minute there was a good chance I was moving back to Idaho, close to them, next minute I'm going more than twice as far away as before."

She was stunned that he'd driven all that way so he could talk with his family face-to-face. It was…amazing. Heartwarming. No wonder he'd looked red-eyed and exhausted yesterday. And there was more to it than met the eye, she was sure. There was something he still hadn't told her. "You left Colorado when?"

"A week ago. Reached my parents Wednesday, left again Friday, to come east. Couldn't quite make it the whole way by Sunday night. I'd run out of toothpicks."

"Toothpicks?"

"For propping my eyelids open. So I crashed at a motel in Syracuse. Told you I was tired yesterday."

"I could see you were."

"I apologized for it, in fact."

"Mac, why was it so important to talk to your family face-to-face?" There was something going on here; she knew it down to her bones.

Silence. Then, "Why is it so important for you not to talk to yours?"

"I'm not *not* talking to them."

"I think you are."

"Okay, then, I want to wait till I have answers for them, is all."

"You honestly think that having a baby is mainly about having answers?"

"Well, part of it is, this early on."

"No, it's not! There are no answers!" His voice rose. "A baby isn't a curveball that you shape up to hit. It isn't an inconvenience that you manage. Or an accessory that you use to make fashion statements."

"Mac, I want this baby. I've said that. What have I said or done to make you think I'm treating it like an inconvenience or an accessory?" She sat up, but kept the sheet pulled high.

He ignored her. "It's major. Huge. And it doesn't kick in with the birth, it kicks in long before that."

"How do you know this?"

"How do I *know?*"

"I mean, I—I'm not arguing." She felt the faltering in her voice and didn't understand herself. She was normally pretty comfortable with other people's opinions about her, and pretty direct about it. How did Mac manage to make her doubt everything, just with that blazing, black-eyed glare? "It is major. You're right. It is huge. It has kicked in. But why do you say it as if you know it so well? As if you feel it so personally? You don't have a child, you've told me that. Was that not true? Is there actually some woman in Coeur d'Alene raising your ten-year-old?"

"Of course there isn't," he muttered. "Or I would have told you."

"So what haven't you told me?"

He shook his head and pressed his lips together, stuck his feet into his shoes. She heard the sound of an engine, and knew that this time it was the delivery truck she'd been waiting for.

"There's something you're not telling me, Mac," she repeated. "So you'd better think about how you're *going* to tell me, because it's important. I can see that in every line of your body and every breath you take. But right now I have to go tell these guys where to unload."

"I'll go tell them. You get dressed. Restaurant is that nice wooden building with the deck over by the lake, right?"

"I'll be out in a minute."

"After they've gone, we'll talk. You're right. It's due." The words sounded ominous.

She began scrambling into her clothes, hearing his feet thump down the stairs, and then male voices over the idling of a truck engine as he directed the driver across to the restaurant. The staff entrance and service hatch leading to the basement storage rooms were both locked, so she grabbed the keys from the office, along with a jacket because there was snow in the forecast and it was turning cold. Moments later Lee was supervising the unloading of half a truckful of boxes of wine and beer and spirits.

"Where does it all go?" Mac asked her, and when she showed him the cellar room, he started ferrying the boxes into it and stacking them, shaking his head when she suggested they could be stacked properly later. "That doesn't make sense."

"For now we just need to get everything off the truck so we don't keep the driver waiting."

"That means we end up lifting every box twice," he pointed out. "I'll do it now."

"In that case, I'll help."

"No, you won't."

"Mac, I can lift a carton with six bottles in it. You know how fit I am."

He looked at her and she could see the struggle going on within. Finally, he answered, "The small cartons. I don't know why you have to make it into a big deal."

"I'm not the one doing that."

"Maybe not," he grunted, and then they both let it go because it was obvious that they needed to talk this out, and that couldn't happen yet.

They worked without speaking to each other, although they both tried to disguise the silence between them with occasional chatty remarks to the truck driver. Lee was intensely aware of the way Mac worked, hefting each box onto one strong shoulder, balancing it there and then heaving it into position, walking tall and steady, with his butt tight and well-muscled and drawing her gaze.

He'd taken off his jacket and rolled the sleeves of the button-down shirt, but he wasn't really dressed for this. He should be in a polo shirt and jeans. He shouldn't be doing this at all, really, but that was one of the things she liked about him. He always pitched in, whether it was drying dishes or sweeping snow from the steps of the Narmans' huge house.

It seemed like an hour before the truck finally drove away, but it wasn't really. More like fifteen minutes, but it was painfully slow the way those minutes ticked by. Lee locked the service hatch and the staff door and shoved the keys in her jacket pocket, then turned, to find Mac shifting on his feet, watching her.

"Let's go for a walk," he said. "Show me the lake."

"You want to see the lake? Now?"

"I want to talk. Might as well walk. I hate doing this stuff sitting on a couch, or whatever. Much rather do it outside."

She knew what he meant. They had it in common, this need for air and space. "A walk would be good."

They both put their hands in their pockets and stumped along with cold ears. Clouds had come over and the air was getting chillier by the minute. It would be snowing within the next hour. She took him along the new walkway that led between the cabins and out to the beach and boat dock, and they rambled close to the water, where tiny waves lapped the rocks and sand.

Mac didn't say anything at first, and since she didn't know what question to ask him to start this conversation, she didn't say anything, either.

"You're not nagging," he observed.

"No, I don't seem to be, do I?"

"Thanks. Like that about you."

"You're welcome. I think."

They covered several more yards in silence.

"I don't have a child," he suddenly said. "But I thought I was going to, once."

"You thought?"

"I had a girlfriend, Sloane. This is six years ago." He thought for a moment. "Seven years, almost. Wow." His voice dropped as if he was talking to himself. "Yes, very soon it'll be seven years…." His tone changed again. "I was twenty-five, she was twenty-two. We slipped up… No, that's not really it. She said to leave the contraception to her, but she kept forgetting to take her pill. I'm not telling this right. At all. But it's hard." He made a sound of deep frustration.

"It's okay." Lee thought about taking his arm, but he still had both hands pushed deep in his pockets. They reached a rocky promontory jutting out into the lake, too hard to climb around unless you'd come prepared, which they hadn't. They turned back in the opposite direction, and he began to speak again.

"She was a professional athlete, a pro surfer, but she loved to snowboard, too. That's how we met, on a mountain. She was thinking of switching, really wanted to do both, which was overambitious for a start."

"Sounds it." Lee knew a few people who'd been torn between surfing and boarding, but all of them had had to choose one to focus on.

"Anyhow, Sloane got pregnant, and she was an overachiever and the most stubborn person I've ever met. She honestly thought she could just cruise through the pregnancy and not change anything about her life or her plans, and it wouldn't make a difference. She didn't want to get married. I mean, it didn't even come up. My parents would have liked it 'for the baby's sake,' they said. But I knew it would have been a disaster. Sloane would have pushed against something that conventional, every step of the way."

"Did your parents like her?"

"They liked her as a person. They liked her company. Or maybe they pretended well. But her attitude scared them. Hell, it scared me! She thought she was going to stay on the pro surfing tour with a baby, keep boarding on the side. She wouldn't slow down. *Would not.* I don't know how she was thinking we'd do it. That I'd travel with her and take care of the baby when she was surfing?"

Mac and Lee reached Spruce Bay's wooden dock, and he turned and stepped onto it, then walked out to the end and leaned on the rail. The water made musical lapping and slapping sounds against the thick supporting posts. The resort's boats were still put away for winter, as were most others at various marinas and docks, and the lake was quiet. Just one small motorboat nosed its way around an island, maybe the same boat Lee had heard earlier and thought for a moment was the delivery truck. She stood beside Mac and leaned on the rail, too.

"I tried to get her to think about the practicalities," he said, "but she just kept saying she didn't want to raise a baby in suburbia, and that women have carried their babies on their backs for thousands of years, and all kinds of other stuff. She said we didn't need a crib, the baby could sleep with us. We didn't need a stroller, we'd use one of those baby slings. She yelled at me for underestimating her capability, for limiting my vision of our lives. She kept insisting that I would see that she was right once the baby was born." He shook his head and stared down at the water. "Anyhow, it never got to that point."

Lee could barely breathe. "What happened, Mac?"

"She wouldn't stop boarding. She was six months pregnant and she was still saying that a woman's body was made to cradle and protect the pregnancy, and nothing would go wrong. She was doing halfpipe one day…."

Lee suddenly flashed back to that time in Colorado last month when they'd eaten hot dogs for lunch, watching the Men's Superpipe snowboarding. She remembered Mac's ambivalence, his talk of "risk minimization," and felt very scared about what was coming next.

"I was there," he said. "But I didn't argue."

"You blame yourself for that," she stated quietly.

"Sometimes. I keep thinking if I'd…" He sighed and shook his head, the air harsh between his teeth. "But I'd given up by then. Knew if I'd tried to get her to stop she would have gone all out to prove her point even harder. Gone faster. Done bigger tricks. She was like that." He leaned lower on the rail and watched the lake some more. It was in gray shadow now, and the snow wasn't far away. "She was so driven and so, so stubborn."

A bit like you, his momentary silence seemed to say. "Stubborn" Lee probably agreed with. "Driven," she wasn't so sure.

"But maybe I should have…I don't know…forced her somehow. Forced her off that mountain."

"Wouldn't she have fought you?"

"Yeah. She would have. But still…" He paused for a moment, and Lee could feel him revisiting all the scenarios that hadn't happened, all the actions he hadn't taken.

"Anyhow, she had a pretty hard fall," he went on. "Got straight back on her feet and said she was fine, just bruised. Wouldn't get herself checked out. Said she could still feel the baby moving, and that everything was okay. I don't know if she really could feel anything or if it was just wishful thinking. But I wouldn't let it go and she yelled at me about it, then finally, the next day, we went to the doctor and the baby wasn't moving. It was—" He didn't say it. Took a slow breath. "They had to induce labor."

"Oh, Mac!" Lee had a lump in her throat. He sounded so broken.

"And it was a boy, and he was perfect. Tiny. And he could have been all right. He would have been, if she hadn't gone boarding that day. There's a chance he could have lived, even after the fall. If she really had felt him moving, maybe if she'd gotten some attention right away, they could have…I mean, they can work miracles in medicine now…." He stopped. "I don't know. I'll never know."

"Mac…" Lee said again.

"Mom and Dad have told me over and over not to do this to myself, not to think about those ifs and maybes, and I'm getting a lot better at it. At distracting myself. But sometimes I can't stop them, in my head."

"No, of course." She wondered about the "distracting myself" part—about making love an hour ago, upstairs. A distraction? "You broke up?" she asked.

"Of course we did. How could we have survived something like that? Last week, after you told me about the pregnancy, I knew I couldn't just hit my parents with the news on the phone. It brings up so much stuff for them, as well as for me. They had to sit on the sidelines, watching the whole disaster unfold. And they were grieving, too. They lost a grandchild."

"Where is Sloane now?" Lee ached for him, and all she could come out with was these questions, short and practical. She didn't know what else to say.

"Still surfing, last time I heard. Based in Hawaii. I don't hear from her. Well, a couple of phone calls and emails, every once in a while. I don't want to hear from her, hate when she gets in touch."

"Of course."

"So if I push you about taking care of yourself, that's why. If I push you sometimes. If I bulldoze you, or hang over you. If I'm treating this whole pregnancy thing like a big deal, like something complicated, that's why."

"I'm not Sloane."

"No, but you're a professional athlete, effectively, just like she was."

"I'm not that driven. I'm not a competitor. I just like to stay active in the fresh air."

"What are you going to do about that?"

"I teach skiing, remember? The season's almost over now, and the baby's due at the beginning of fall."

"That's not an answer. You mountain guide in the summer. You teach rock climbing, too."

"You think I plan to still be teaching rock climbing when I'm six months pregnant? What have I said that you would make such an assumption?"

"I'm just asking, Lee."

"And I'm telling you. I'm not Sloane."

"Do you not think I have the right to ask, in this situation?"

"You have the right to ask, but not the right to assume."

He ignored her. "I had no control over what Sloane did with her body, even though the baby she was carrying was mine as much as it was hers. Even though I *knew* she was being pigheaded and unrealistic, and her doctor agreed with me."

"I'll listen to the doctor, Mac."

But he was beyond hearing her, right now. "And our child died before he was even born. She was so big on living life to the full, and yet our son never got to live life at all, because Sloane had some crazy point to prove, and it was horrible. Really horrible. For a long time. The loss and grief, all mixed up with guilt and anger and denial and recriminations, including my parents telling me to be more careful about who I dated next time. I need to know how you feel about that stuff, what your plans are. I have a right to ask."

He turned to her with those blazing eyes and she felt as if he was so far ahead of her, emotionally, that she didn't know how to catch up. He'd stripped himself raw, talking about this, and in return she wanted to protect herself, shrink back into herself and not face the challenge.

And yet she had to.

It was vital for both of them.

Vital for all three of them.

Instinctively, she flattened her hand against her lower stomach, where there was a growing, living baby she couldn't yet feel, and took a big breath. "You do. You have every right to ask," she repeated. "I'm hurting for you, Mac, and I don't know how to show you that, or what words to use. I don't know how to tell you I'd never do what she did. But I never would. I *never* would." Her voice cracked, and she couldn't think of how to say it any better.

The first snowflakes began to fall. She watched them feathering Mac's bare, dark head. He wasn't speaking, but just looking at her, trying to read her soul.

"Is that good enough?" she asked, in a whisper.

"Good enough?"

"I don't know how else to make you believe it. Is this why you're here? Why you drove forty hours? To make sure I keep our baby safe?"

"If you want to say it like that. I'm here because it is *our* baby, not just yours. Sloane always acted like it was hers. And that was even worse after we lost it. She closed up. Her armor was so thick. Fending off the blame. Angry with me. As if that protected her from her own grief and guilt. And then crying on the phone a couple times a year, expecting me to make her feel better. As if I didn't feel as bad. Or worse." He shook his head.

Couldn't talk about it anymore.

Lee understood that.

She felt the hurt in him once more, almost as if it was a pain in her own body. She laid a hand on his shoulder and stepped against him. The snow came faster, settling on them quicker than it could melt. "I won't shut you out, Mac, I promise. I'll listen when you talk. I'll understand if you come on a bit too strong. We'll navigate this somehow. We'll have a baby. We won't have a mess. As far as anyone can, I promise that."

"Good." He pulled her closer and rested his chin on the top of her head. She could hear the scratchiness in his voice, and feel the tension making his muscles quiver. "I promise it, too."

They stood there in each other's arms, not talking anymore, just holding each other, until Lee's ears ached and her hair was thick with droplets of snowmelt.

Chapter Ten

Mary Jane arrived home from her spa vacation in Vermont at lunchtime the next day.

Mac was sitting in the office making calls on his cell phone to friends and contacts at ski schools and management headquarters in the region, while Lee browsed the computer, looking at all the changes Daisy had made to the Spruce Bay website—their reservation system, their restaurant menu, their specials packages and various other things. It all looked great, so much more up-to-date than the tired old place it had been before Mom and Dad retired.

Lee heard Mary Jane's car, and then saw it zoom up to a parking spot in front of the office and come to a sudden halt, making a slightly strange noise in its engine before Mary Jane turned it off. She jumped out, grabbed her bags from the trunk, bounced up the steps and flung open the door, looking trim and relaxed and energized, with her brown hair full of golden highlights and swinging around her face. "Hey...I'm back!"

At which point Lee registered just how at home Mac looked here in the office. He was rocked back in a swivel chair with his feet on the spare desk and one hand cradling the back of his neck, saying into the phone, "So could I come up and take a look around? Like, soon?"

"Oh," said Mary Jane, taking him in.

The running shoes.

The rolled shirtsleeves.

And possibly also the olive skin, black eyes and very nice arm muscles, all of which Lee had been very much enjoying since yesterday.

She pushed back from the computer and came around the main desk to give Mary Jane a hug and take one of her bags. "Um, that's Mac," she said a little awkwardly, sticking a thumb in his direction.

"Good to meet you, Mac," said Mary Jane, in a very level tone.

He was still on the phone, listening and saying, "Uh-huh," at intervals, but he gave her a wave and a nod and a smile.

"So does he live here or work here?" she murmured.

"Neither."

But Lee couldn't blame her sister for the question. The whole office exuded an atmosphere of casual— and possibly quite sexy—familiarity between the two of them.

Yesterday, with the snow thickening in the air around them and beginning to settle on the ground, they'd walked back from the lake hugged close in each other's arms. He'd said just before they went inside, "I really hit you with all of that, didn't I? Like, wham, full in the face."

"You needed to. I needed to hear it. Thank you."

"It probably explains a few things." He'd spoken slowly. "Couple of times where I might have overreacted."

"It does," she agreed.

"Are we okay now?"

"How okay do you mean?"

"I don't understand the question," he said.

"We kind of broke up yesterday," she reminded him. "And then this morning we...well, did the usual."

"Doesn't seem like we're broken up, then, does it?" he suggested. He cupped her butt possessively.

"No."

"Do you want to be broken up?" he asked.

"No. I like you. I really like being with you. I can think of way worse people to be having a baby with than you." As a declaration of undying love, it fell possibly just a little short, but she was cautious about stuff like this, and for obvious reasons, so was he.

Nearly eleven years ago, she'd gotten to within four days of a big wedding to the man who'd just married her sister, and she shuddered to think what would have happened to them all if the wedding had gone ahead. Would Tucker and Daisy have fallen into a hot affair behind her back? Would Lee herself have realized the marriage was a mistake, and run two thousand miles, leaving a huge mess behind her? She'd run two thousand miles anyhow, even without the wedding taking place, because she'd needed a lot of distance in order to regroup.

She found it incredibly scary to think back on herself and Tucker, and how close they'd come to making that mess. To have let somebody that near to her and then to realize it was wrong was...profoundly unsettling. It shook the very foundations of what she knew about herself. And it was most definitely something she did not want to do more than once, because if she stripped herself emotionally again with the wrong man, for the wrong reasons, she wasn't sure she'd ever get her confidence back.

"Same back at you, sugar," Mac had answered cheerfully, in the snow. If he thought her declaration fell short, he wasn't showing it. Maybe he needed as much caution as she did.

"Except don't call me that again," she'd told him.

"Not even at a romantic moment like this?"

"Nope."

"Okay, noted."

The rest of the day—and all of the night—had this same mood to it. A little wistful and quiet at times, with a solemn undercurrent because of what he'd shared. But tender, too.

Funny.

Easy.

Close.

And now Mary Jane had walked right into it, and didn't know what was going on. "Lee, I've only been gone three days," she said, in the same confidential undertone as before.

"Yes, well, he drove from Colorado via Idaho, and I didn't know he was coming till he got here."

Her sister read her like a book, and concluded, "But you're glad he did."

"Um, yes," she admitted. Scarily glad, now that they'd dealt with a few difficult things.

Mac ended his call. He took his feet off the spare desk and planted them on the floor. "Good to meet you, too, Mary Jane." He stood up and came over and stuck out his hand, leaning in to hug her and pat her on the back and almost kiss her cheek at the same time—the kind of all-purpose greeting a man gave to a woman he didn't know that well, or at all, but he had reason to think he was going to become fond of in the future. "Tell her," he said to Lee.

"Tell me what?"

"Tell her why I'm here, what this is about."

Lee bristled a little at this, but tried not to let it show. "I'll get to that in a minute," she answered brightly.

Was it her problem? She honestly didn't know. The legacy of the baby he and Sloane had lost hung heavy over him still, and she understood that. But his words seemed to her like an order, and she didn't think their talk yesterday and their closeness after it had given him that right.

He was involved, yes. They were sharing this, were both committed to making this pregnancy work after his terrible experience with Sloane and his lost child, but that didn't mean he got to dictate the timing and pace on everything.

And he was acting as if the baby was the only thing that mattered. The announcement he was looking for would go, "Guess what, we're having a baby," not, "Guess what, I have a boyfriend," and it seemed out of balance.

If they were *together,* which they seemed to be, then that was a pretty important announcement, too, wasn't it?

"Tell me what?" Mary Jane repeated.

"Want some lunch, you two?" Lee kept the brightness, even though she wasn't blind to Mac's frowning.

"Just say it, Lee," he growled. "Or if you don't, I will. Putting it off doesn't help."

Now she was really bristling. "Go ahead, then."

But don't expect me to make it into a double act.

Apparently, he didn't read that second bit, although she'd signaled it quite clearly with her eyes.

"She's pregnant," he said.

Because, you know, it wouldn't do to squander any unnecessary syllables. Those are in short supply.

He went on, "That's why she came east, Mary Jane. For family support. And I followed her, because I didn't want her doing this—having the baby—on her own."

There was a moment of stunned silence before Mary Jane inhaled sharply. "Oh. Oh, wow! Oh, oh, oh, wow! Lee! Wow! *Wow!*"

"You're overusing that word a little, sis." Her flippant protest got lost in Mary Jane's hug, huge and warm.

"You really are? Having a baby?"

"I really am."

"Wow! How far along?"

"Nearly three months. Had a bit of a blip, and didn't realize for a while."

"Oh, wow! I am so happy for you!"

"Thanks." Half a minute ago, Lee had been angry and defiant. Now she was... What? Happy? Yes?

About her sister's reaction, definitely.

"Oh, wow!"

"Careful, Mary Jane." She gave a shaky laugh. "Your limited license for the word *wow* is seriously about to expire."

"Oh, stop!" Mary Jane drew back a little and looked Lee full in the face, with tears in her eyes, and beaming. "I'm not allowed to be happy? This isn't good news? I'm going to be an aunt!"

Okay, maybe Lee had some tears in the pipeline, too. "Yes, it's good news," she said, and realized it was the first time she'd thought of it that way—as something blessed and wonderful to announce to everybody and be congratulated about.

She'd made her vow to her baby's living heartbeat, and she'd made promises to Mac about her commitment and her care, but those had been private things. Serious things. Decisions, not celebrations.

Telling people was going to be very different.

Telling Mary Jane was already very different to what Lee had thought it would be. For a start, she hadn't necessarily thought her sister would be happy, since it was a pretty open secret in the Cherry family that Mary Jane would love a family—a traditional one, starting with a husband and a white wedding and going from there.

But clearly she was happy—generously, excitedly happy—and it was a revelation. It was fantastic!

Mac, too, kept insisting that this pregnancy was complicated and momentous and serious, and he was right, it was. But it was also joyous and life-affirming and magical, and neither he nor Lee had really thought about that yet.

They hadn't celebrated, and here was Mary Jane, who could have felt jealous and left out, showing them how.

She was still sparkling. "So…there's obviously so much to talk about. I'm going to be Aunt Mary Jane! Mac, it's so great to meet you! Wow—sorry, another one. But I never thought my first meeting with my sister's new man would come hand in hand with a pregnancy announcement. We should sit down and have lunch, and really celebrate. Shall I throw something together?"

"We don't have to have a big lunch, Mary Jane," Lee said.

"Well, I do, because I'm telling you, they did *not* believe in breakfast at that spa. It's one o'clock in the afternoon and I've had nothing but fruit."

"You look great, though. It can't have been too spartan there."

"No, it wasn't. Gorgeous fruit, I should have said. And the massage was fabulous, and the facials, and the mud wrap, and the yoga and movement classes. And the silent retreat."

"You fit all that into three days?"

"And I slept like a log. The pillows! Please let me make us lunch."

"Go for it, if you want," Lee said, laughing again.

"I'll call you when it's ready," Mary Jane promised. "You look busy in here. Then we'll talk more. I want to hear all the details." She picked up her bags again, and headed up the stairs.

When she'd gone, Mac repeated wryly, "She wants to hear all the details."

Lee's response was cautious. "Well, we can give her a few of them."

"I'm going to be the third wheel." He stood up, with his jaw set square, and reached for the truck keys in his pocket. "You need to do this sister to sister."

Lee looked at the keys, but couldn't disagree. "I think you're right." She felt relieved, in fact. One of them would be the third wheel, but she wasn't convinced it would be Mac. Mary Jane, maybe.

Or me...

Sandwiched in between one thrilled sister and one overprotective father-to-be, whom she hadn't known nearly long enough. Whom she loved being close to, but—

But what?

She couldn't do this all at once. Become a committed relationship partner, and a glowing future mom, and an indoor manager sitting at a desk and being super cautious with her body, when four months ago she'd been single and independent and out in the open air all day, with no one's needs to consult but her own, nothing to work out about her reasons for doing the things she did.

Mac seemed so totally focused on the baby, but there was a lot more going on than just that.

"Go tell her it's two for lunch, not three," he said. "I'm driving up to Whiteface this afternoon to take a look around, if that's okay." He came over and gave Lee a kiss, then held her lightly. The air seemed to heat and vibrate with their connection, the way it always did. Which was wonderful, but there was a part of her that found so much of this far too overwhelming, and was really glad he had somewhere to go right now.

"Of course it's okay," she told him, meaning it.

"I have a friend working there who thinks he can find some people for me to talk to about a job."

"That was the phone call, just now?"

"Yes, did you hear?"

"Mary Jane arrived. I was distracted. Her car's making a weird noise. Heard you ask if you could come up and take a look around. And you looked happy. You're obviously hoping something will pan out up there."

"Don't like too much downtime."

"Me, neither."

"So it's okay? We're okay?" He touched the ball of his thumb to her lower lip, then bent to kiss her quickly.

"Mary Jane is going to want to get to know you. That's clear. But if she and I can have some time together first, it's probably for the best."

"Mac's not staying," she told Mary Jane upstairs, a minute later.

"Oh. How come?" She was standing in the kitchen, slicing mushrooms and chopping bacon.

"He's driving up to Whiteface to talk to a couple of people about a job."

"Whiteface? He'd be two hours from here, if he was

working there. That's a big commute, especially in winter."

"Maybe he wouldn't commute. Maybe he'd live there."

"Live there? This isn't totally making sense to me, Lee." Her sister slid the heaps of mushroom and bacon into a pan slicked with olive oil. "He's moving east. Which means you're moving east, too, doesn't it?"

"Whatcha making?"

"Mushroom and bacon frittata, with salad on the side. Is that okay?"

"Sounds great."

"You need to eat right," Mary Jane announced. "Fiber and vitamins."

"Duh, do I? I was planning a six-month junk food spree."

"You didn't answer my question about moving east, Lee, don't think I didn't notice. You're looking for something at Whiteface, too? How are you going to manage all of this? Are you getting married? You haven't even mentioned him till now. Has it been going on long?"

"Mary Jane, I'm about to pass out from a question overdose."

"So start answering some of them." She grabbed a box of eggs and a bag of lettuce from the refrigerator.

"Yes, I've moved back east. I didn't tell you guys last week that I was making it permanent, because there was a pretty nice wedding happening here last weekend and I didn't want to distract from it. Bad enough I was the ex-fiancée and a bridesmaid, both at the same time."

"Tucker and Daisy didn't give that a thought. To them it's ancient history."

"I could tell." Lee had a sudden mental slide show of all those moments when the bridal couple couldn't look at anyone but each other. "It was great. And ancient history for me, too. No, I'm not looking for something at Whiteface. I'm wondering about living here, helping run the resort. We need to have a proper Cherry sisters meeting about that, because I don't know if there's a place for me here. What was the next question?"

"Can't remember. Are you getting married, maybe?"

"No, we're not getting married. We've only known each other for three months."

"You got pregnant a minute after you met?"

"The way doctors count it—which, if you didn't know, is from first day of your last period, not the date of actual conception—I got pregnant *before* we met."

"That strikes me as a little rash."

"It was apparently a technical issue involving latex. Don't ask."

"Yeah, way too much information."

"I'm not sure yet how I'm going to manage. Maybe I've come rushing home here for no good reason." Because Mac had come rushing, too, and it was complicating things in ways she didn't fully understand. "The baby wasn't planned. Obviously."

"Obviously. But you're happy about it." Suddenly, Mary Jane got serious. "I really, really need to know that you're happy about it, Lee." She turned away from the stove and faced her, with a frown on her face and a question in her eyes.

Lee engulfed her sister in a huge hug, and felt the tension in her body. "I'm very happy about it. Scared, but happy. I'm really happy that you're happy, Mary Jane. I loved how excited you got. I loved all the wows, really. Loved them. Oh, shoot, I'm crying."

"So am I." Mary Jane reached behind her and shut off the burner on the stove.

Lee pulled back, wiped tears on a sleeve and looked at her. "Why did you really, really need to know that I'm happy?"

Her sister sighed, took a breath, sighed again and finally got going. "Because if you weren't, then it would be too unfair. I've always wanted marriage and babies, and you've kind of shrugged about it and said, 'Someday...' And now it's happening to you and not me, and if you were still going, 'Huh, I'm not sure I want this,' about it, I might have to hate you."

"Ooh, no, don't do that."

"It's the hardest, hardest thing, watching someone else disdain something that you want desperately yourself." She blinked back more tears. "And we were close as kids, and I don't want to hate you, because now you're back and we can be close again, all three of us, and I'm really excited about that."

Lee laughed, and kept crying at the same time. Possibly a hormone thing. "I'm excited about it, too."

"Have some tissues." Mary Jane passed the box from the top of the refrigerator.

"Thanks." They both blinked and sniffed. "Is there a place for me here, Mary Jane? Working the reservations system, or manning the office? Helping Daisy in the restaurant?"

"Of course there's a place for you! Probably six places, over the summer. I was going to have to hire someone for the office, because I can't be everywhere at once and our summer reservations are already well up on last year."

"That's what I hoped—that I could do, instead of new staff."

"You won't 'do.' You'll be fabulous. Didn't we have

fun here when we were kids? Don't you remember how much everyone had fun here?"

"I do!"

"And the remodel has been brilliant, don't you think? I can't wait for summer."

"Me, too."

They laughed and sighed and felt better.

Mary Jane picked up on the practicalities again, a few moments later. "So you'll live here. And Mac might be two hours away. Doesn't that bother you?"

"Nope."

"Does it bother you that it doesn't bother you?"

"Not that, either."

Mary Jane's shrug was highly expressive as she turned back to the stove and clicked the gas burner back on. Lee had never realized how much an older sister's shoulders could say.

"Why do you think it should bother me?" She watched Mary Jane stirring the mushrooms and bacon. Her stirring attained a pretty impressive level of communication, also.

"Did I say that?" She put down the spoon and began cracking eggs into a bowl. "Want to wash the lettuce?"

"Sure." Lee went to the sink, and Mary Jane pulled a salad spinner out of a cupboard and handed it to her. Lee ran water over the lettuce, then put the lid on the spinner and started it whirring around, telling her sister above the humming sound, "You didn't have to say it, Mary Jane. Just asking the question made it obvious. Two hours isn't that far. We'll still see each other. As much as we want."

"Or as little."

"That, too."

"That, too," Mary Jane echoed, the tone so wooden you could have made furniture out of it.

"It's good that we can be flexible about it. We're not painting ourselves into any kind of corner. Things can evolve."

"Evolve." More furniture. A whole bedroom set.

"Yes." She turned the spinner handle faster, and the noise of it and the sizzling bacon made it hard to keep talking.

Which was good, because Lee thought they were done.

Chapter Eleven

Mac drove back from Whiteface in the dark. It wasn't an easy trip, half of it on minor mountain roads until the merge onto I-87 South.

And even the interstate could get pretty bad in a storm, this far north, with snow slowing the drive or blocking the roads.

Hell of a commute from Lake George.

The afternoon had gone very well, though, better than he'd hoped. There was a job for him if he wanted it, and a lead on accommodation, as well. The job started in two and a half weeks, and the rental on the small house in the town of Jay was open from the beginning of May, just over a month away. He'd seen a couple photos of the place, and would have to drive up there again within the next couple days if he wanted to see it properly before committing to a lease. He'd lose it if he wasn't fast.

If he took it, that would take care of the commuting problem. Jay was half an hour from Whiteface.

But it was an hour and twenty minutes from Lee.

He wondered how thoroughly she and Mary Jane had covered the pregnancy and the relationship, over lunch. What had they said after he left? He knew Lee hadn't been happy about the way he'd announced it, but he wasn't going to be sidelined, and he wasn't going to deal with any pretense that it wasn't happening.

He'd done that.

Been there.

Been through it.

All the crazy stuff about not needing to buy a crib or a stroller or even a diaper bag, because all that paraphernalia would just tie them down. And when Sloane *had* wanted to talk about it happening, about actually having a baby in their lives, there'd always been the blithe assumption that you made a child in your own image, that the baby would be exactly who and what you wanted it to be.

They'd had to name him for his funeral, and they'd called him Kelly after the surfing champion, but when he was just a tiny being of unknown gender inside her, Sloane had called him Peanut. She used to say that Peanut, female or male, was going to be an Olympic snowboarding gold medal winner. "The kid'll practically have been born on a board. It'll be a natural. What choice will it have?" she used to say, half joking, half not.

And in a horrible way it was true: little baby Kelly practically had been born on a board. Had died on a board. Under a board. Slammed against a board.

Hell!

It's happening. Lee and I are having a baby.

Why does it have to happen like this?

There was a part of Mac that wanted to demand that he and Lee get married, so that he would have more control. He could stand back and look at that piece of himself, with all its fear and bullishness, and sometimes he had to fight so hard not to give in to it.

Marry me, Lee.

Marry me, damn it, so I can force the right choices on you and you can't argue.

As if that was a good reason for a marriage.

As if marriage gave you that kind of control, anyhow.

It scared him that he wanted it—that he wanted to turn into some historical throwback who didn't want his wife to vote or work or even speak, unless it was in complete agreement with himself.

He wasn't that person, but he had to fight not to want to be.

It would be the worst, most disastrous thing in the world if he and Lee got married when he was feeling this way. She might be thinking about the *M* word, too, but he very much doubted she would have that kind of a marriage in mind.

Back at his little cottage, he called her, needing to get back to the relationship they really had, not the one half of him wanted. Back to the relationship where they laughed and made love, and understood so much about each other, and had fun together.

"Wanna come over and see my place?" he said to her on the phone, dropping his voice to the low, intimate pitch she could give back to him with extra spice. "It's not quite an eleven million dollar Aspen mansion, but it's close. One bathroom instead of seven and no Jacuzzi, but that's a detail."

"I love the way you're selling it." Yes, *that* pitch, with a laugh in it. "How'd it go at Whiteface?"

"Talk when you get here." He was smiling like an idiot, into the phone.

"Didn't say I was coming, did I?"

"Are you coming?"

"Car keys in my hand."

"Wait, have you eaten?"

"No, that big lunch of Mary Jane's filled me up. I'm only just getting hungry now. Thought I'd wait to see if you called."

"And I did," he said.

"You did," she agreed. "Want me to pick up some takeout on my way? Pizza place might be open."

"Pizza is good. You know what I like."

"Happens I do, seeing as it's the same as what I like."

"Which is handy."

"I'll be there in half an hour."

Thirty-four minutes later, he heard the slam of a car door above the sound of the TV, and there she was, balancing a pizza box on the flat of her hand. Her cheeks were pink in the cold and she'd twisted her dark-caramel hair into a round knot high on the back of her head, so that it left her square jaw clear.

She wore jeans and a close-fitting stretchy top almost the same color as her hair, with a white tank underneath that showed at the neckline, and for the first time he thought he could see the beginnings of a bump, right where the hem of the top slid over the waistband of the jeans. He could definitely see the other two bumps he loved, round and bouncy when she walked.

"Here's your delivery," she said. He loved the shape of her face when she smiled, loved the life in her eyes.

"If it was anything but pizza, I'd probably want to get you naked first."

"The freshness of pizza is sacred, I do agree." She came past him, still balancing the box, and let her free hand trail across his chest, making a promise for later.

The pizza smelled of mushroom and onion and olives and anchovies, and suddenly he was so hungry he thought she should probably have gotten two.

They sat on the couch with the open box on the coffee table in front of them, and demolished all eight slices between two commercial breaks in a crime show, while outside the wind picked up and sleet began to fall. It was so cozy in here, reminding him of those nights in her little janitor apartment in Aspen, back when everything was so simple between them.

How could they possibly get back to that?

Maybe if they pretended… Or if they only talked about… Or if they didn't talk at all, but just…

They couldn't. Nothing was simple now.

"You haven't told me about Whiteface yet," she said, when the pizza was gone.

"Waiting to see who the killer is, first."

"The killer is the wife."

"The wife is too obvious."

"It's a double bluff from the writers. They know we'll think it's too obvious."

She was wrong. It wasn't the wife. It was the girlfriend. Turned out Mac didn't care either way. They had important things to discuss. "Whiteface was good," he said slowly. "I have a job, if I want it, and a house to rent, if I want that."

"And do you want them?" Lee snuggled against him, snaking her arm between his back and the couch and resting her head on his shoulder.

"The job, almost certainly. The house, I'm still thinking."

"Is it nice?"

"From the photos, yes. Have to make up my mind pretty soon." If he turned the rental opportunity down, there might not be anything else as workable for a while. He'd end up staying down here and driving a heck of a lot—four hours a day. But if that meant he had Lee in his bed every night so he could watch over her, maybe it was the best plan. "Not an easy decision, but important. We have to work out which options make sense, and which just don't."

Tempting way to think. Dangerous way to think. What was he planning, here? What did he want, and why did he want it?

"Yeah?" Her chin burrowed into his collarbone.

"We have to be careful about our decisions, both of us," he repeated. She must be thinking along the same lines, surely. There was an elephant in the room, and it had a ring on its finger and was wearing a veil and a white dress. "We can't paint ourselves into a corner."

"How, a corner? I mean, I was thinking about corners myself, but tell me yours."

"End up getting married, out of some feeling that we should." This was the danger, as he saw it.

He'd surprised her. *"Married?"* She sat up, making a cool space between their bodies. He wanted her back. "Where did that come from?"

"You haven't thought about it?"

She looked really shocked. "This is not how two people talk about getting married." She was hugging her elbows, arms crossed over her front, pushing up those breasts he'd been thinking about with such eagerness a few minutes ago.

"I'm talking about *not* getting married, Lee."

"You're talking about it as if it's on the table, one of our options, something we're thinking about, the most appropriate thing to do."

"No, I'm saying it shouldn't be. I'm saying the opposite." He started to sweat, regretting that his thoughts had traveled faster than his mouth, and it had all come out wrong. "That it would be disastrous. That we'd be doing it for all the wrong reasons. Don't you think?

People have a hard enough time *staying* married for the sake of their kids. *Getting* married for that reason in the first place would be...wrong. Really wrong. You have to see that."

She was just looking at him. Eyes narrowed. Shock still on her face. Not happy. Not saying a word.

Finally, the silence between them grew so thick that he had to break it. "What?"

"What do you mean, *what?*"

"C'mon, Lee! You're just sitting there looking at me as if I've grown two new heads, and I'm not trying to be...I don't even know what. Controversial? Hostile? I just think it would be a mistake for us to think about getting married."

She spoke very slowly and patiently, green eyes blazing, and he hated it. "I...have never...ever...mentioned...the word *marriage*. You...are the one...who brought it up. And now you're giving me this argument as if I'm trying to trap you and you have to scramble to get out of the trap, and that is so unfair, and then you're surprised I went a bit speechless."

"So you weren't thinking about it?" Seemed he was very, very wrong about the elephant in the room.

"About getting married? No!"

"About *not* getting married, then."

"Not that, either. I totally agree with you. Or I did. Before you went all 'you have to see that, Lee' on my ass."

Wow. She was angry. For someone who hung around with extreme sports nuts a lot, she wasn't prone to coarse language.

"Of course I freaking see it!" she added. Her eyes were still blazing, and he would have loved the fire in them if it hadn't been directed squarely at him. He wanted to apologize, but didn't quite know what to apologize for.

Sorry I made assumptions about the way women think.

She stood up and rubbed her hand against her breastbone, then muttered, "Ouch, I shouldn't have eaten that pizza so fast." She winced.

"What's up?" he said stupidly.

"Don't feel that great. Heartburn, and…" She headed for the bathroom.

"Wait… Wait!"

"Bad time, Mac." She disappeared into it, and the door slammed behind her.

Hell!

He wasn't that prone to coarse language, either, but there were times when it helped. This seemed to be one of them. He'd started this discussion all wrong. He hadn't even known he was starting a discussion, although he had known they needed one. And now they couldn't finish it. He let fly a few more choice words under his breath, then heard the faucet running hard into the sink. "You okay in there?" he called out.

"Not really. But give me a moment."

"Want me to—?"

"Want you to go outside onto the porch so you don't have to listen."

Yeah, the bathroom door was pretty thin.

He took her seriously, grabbed his jacket and went to stand on the porch, which would be a very pleasant place to sit in a month or two. Now, it offered vistas of sleet falling in darkness, and black trees tossing in wind, and despite the jacket, he was shivering in seconds.

He felt helpless and stupid and slow and wrong. She

was back there in the bathroom, bristling with independence, and he'd just treated her like the opposite of who she was. Who had he really been talking to? Himself? He was the one who kept thinking of the marriage idea and having to argue himself out of it.

Lee was...

Lee was scarily like Sloane in some ways, and it hadn't mattered before, in Colorado, but it was starting to matter now. He knew what she would say if he accused her of it. "I am nothing like that!" She'd already said it, and probably she was right.

But still, there were a few things. Her independence. Her toughness. Her athleticism. He loved those things in a woman. Always had. Before Sloane, too, he'd gone for women like that. Since Sloane, he hadn't gone for anyone very much until Lee. There'd been one woman who was different—feminine and kittenish and all about fashion and celebrity gossip—and that had been so wrong it had lasted all of a week before he came to his senses.

So he liked strong women, and he liked Lee.

But, yeah, she was scaring him. This whole situation was scaring him, and he didn't know what to do. How did he protect his unborn child without damaging his relationship with its mother? How did he learn the difference between realistic caution and good sense, and illogical overreaction?

After a few more minutes, he let himself carefully back inside. The bathroom door was still closed, with Lee behind it. The faucet was still running.

"How are you doing now?" he asked, through the door. He leaned against it, waiting for her answer.

"Better," she said, after a moment. "Out in a minute. Write a memo for me, could you? Pregnant women should not gulp pizza."

"Don't think I'll need to write that one down, will I?"

"True. It's engraved on my memory now, for all time."

The door opened. She looked a bit green and she had a towel bunched in her hand the way a child would hug a teddy. As he watched, she brought it up to her face and wiped her mouth, clearly not for the first time. He could smell toothpaste. For a strong woman, she looked pretty fragile right now, and he just wanted to hold her and soothe her. Rub her back. Bring her tea.

"You okay? Want me to get you something?" He hugged her for a moment, and the air seemed sweet between them. Sweet and magnetic and good. He brushed his lips against the air three inches above her forehead. She was warm and a little shaky, and he wanted to sweep the fallen strands of hair away from her face and kiss the top of her head and murmur, *Shh, it's okay now.*

"Like what?" she said.

"Crackers? Tea?"

"Would you have to go to the store?"

"Yes."

"What time is it?"

"Ten."

"Can't send you to the store this late," she concluded.

"Yes, you can. Of course you can."

"No, it's fine. I'll be okay."

"Will you quit being so stubborn about this stuff? There'll be a convenience store open." He still had his jacket on, and the pickup keys were in the pocket. He let her go and took them out, and the fact that she didn't keep arguing told him she was still feeling pretty bad. "So tell me what you need. Fruit? Soup?"

She sighed, as if she was letting go of something. "Just get everything."

"Everything?"

"Crackers, tea—maybe some herbal and some regular. Bananas, grapes, cans of soup, really salty potato chips."

"You don't know what you want."

"I don't know what's going to help. Haven't had much of a problem with this kind of thing so far. Just a couple of mornings, if I let myself get really tired. Clearly haven't been eating pizza often enough—or fast enough—to spot the correlation. So it's been easy to manage. Thank you," she added, more politely than she needed to. "Seriously. Thank you."

"Sorry about before." *Sorry I scared you off. Sorry you're doing this distancing thing now because of it, with the politeness and all.* "About the marriage thing. You were right. I was arguing with myself. You never brought it up. So I'm sorry."

She nodded. "Mistake. It's okay," and he just went.

When he got back with a bulging grocery bag about twenty minutes later, she was curled up on the couch wearing one of his sweaters, a big, bulky gray thing with sleeves that reached past her fingertips. "You could have turned the heating up," he told her gently.

"Not cold. Just needed the comfort."

"Oh. Okay." And she'd gotten the comfort from something of his. Once more, stronger than ever, he felt this crazy rush of tenderness and protectiveness that he didn't dare admit to because of what it might trigger in her reaction. "So what do you want, out of this lot?" he said quickly.

"Um, tea? Regular tea. Weak. A splash of milk. Just

something hot I can sip. And maybe crackers, if you got them."

"I did. Water crackers. Very plain."

"Perfect."

"Tea is coming right up." He put the bag down on the counter in the kitchen that was really just an extension of the living area.

With the TV running another crime show in the background, she watched him boil water, open the box of tea bags and find a mug. A very ugly mug.

"Could lend you some better than those," she offered.

"Might take you up on that, if I sign a lease on— Hey, we haven't really talked about this yet, and I need to, to make a decision. We got distracted."

"We did."

"I'm sorry."

"Me, too," she said slowly. "It was both of us. It wasn't just you. It probably wasn't you at all. And you're right, we haven't really talked about the job or the house."

"It's not furnished. That's the downside."

"And the upside?" She snuggled deeper into the couch and kept watching him at work in the kitchen.

"Half an hour from the mountain, less expensive than I feared."

"Apart from the expense of buying furniture."

"There is that."

"We don't own a lot, either of us, do we?"

"Nope."

They looked at each other. The kettle began to whistle. He poured water into the mug and waited for her to say the things he'd heard before—that you didn't need a whole baby store full of gear, that the whole idea was just a marketing ploy, a trap for new parents.

"It's not that we're poor," he said, because he wasn't. He'd actually saved quite a lot.

She nodded. "Or that we're channeling John Lennon and imagining no possessions. We just haven't needed *stuff,* either of us, till now."

"Till now?"

"Mac, I'm going to be honest with you." She gave a sly, wicked smile, suddenly. "I'm planning to shop. Don't want my baby…our baby…sleeping in a drawer."

Sloane had said the exact opposite.

He laughed. Sheer relief, really.

"What's funny?"

"Nothing." He added very carefully, because he wasn't sure how she'd take it. "Just feeling happy about all of this, that's all."

She grinned at him. "You know what? I am, too…."

It was a very nice night, in the end.

Chapter Twelve

On Friday, Lee drove north with Mac to look at the house available for rent. It was a plain little log cabin, but the bathroom and kitchen had both been updated, it had a pretty deck out back, and it had that indefinable good feeling about it that you couldn't pick up on from an internet photo tour. The furniture currently in place belonged to the tenant who was moving out at the end of April, but Mac would probably acquire similar things—simple, comfortable, no clutter.

"Think I should take it?" he asked her. "Gotta make a decision today, because there's someone else interested. The Realtor's only holding it for me as a favor, because he's the brother of the friend who put me in touch with him."

Mac and Lee looked at each other, and it felt like standing on the edge of a cliff. Scary and not safe, a kind of vertigo that made them dizzy. If he didn't take it, where would he live instead? How much would the physical distance between them—or lack of it—dictate where their relationship went?

"Take it," Lee said. Her heart was beating faster. "How long's the lease?"

"Six months."

Six months. Her due date was almost exactly six months away. Looked at from some angles, this seemed like a long time. Six months away was on the far side of summer, and they still weren't really even into spring. At Spruce Bay, she and Daisy and Mary Jane had a whole season of resort guests and restaurant meals and pool cleaning to get through.

From another angle, six months was no time at all. It was only twice the time she'd known Mac. It was only about six weeks longer than an Aspen ski season. It was only the time it took for a baby to grow from three inches to twenty.

"Renewable," Mac added, about the lease. "So that shouldn't be a problem."

Was he thinking about her due date, too? That he wouldn't want to have to find a new place around then?

They'd been wonderfully at ease with each other since Wednesday night, after the blowup over the marriage idea. He shouldn't have said it that way, as if marriage was a trap she was setting for him. But in response she'd reacted too strongly, so they were both at fault, and it seemed they were both clearer, now, on where they stood.

They didn't want to get married.

Decision number one.

Which sort of suggested there was another decision to make, or more likely quite a few of them, but by unspoken agreement, neither of them was pushing on any of those. It felt like a relief, because she hated that the baby was creating all this pressure. Even more, she hated that they might come to blame the baby for that.

The risk of doing such a thing to her innocent child really horrified her, because she didn't need personal experience to know that something like that could haunt and warp a person for life.

"Take it," Lee repeated. "And I'll help you shop for furniture, if you want."

"We could have fun with that. Testing mattresses."

"And rugs."

"And couches."

They smiled at each other, and drove directly to the Realtor so that Mac could sign the lease. Lee thought it might be pretty nice to be driving up here all summer when they each had some time off. They could eat breakfast and barbecue out on the deck. Put towels down and bask in the sun. Sleep late.

If Mac drove south to see her, they could go boating on the lake, or take a picnic and go for a hike in the woods. Pick wild blueberries on Prospect Mountain. Go to her prenatal appointments.

Hmm. Why did that last one not seem to fit?

On Sunday afternoon, Daisy and Tucker were due back from their weeklong honeymoon in the Bahamas. Mac had gone up to Whiteface again today, with the intention of hopping on skis for a while and getting to know the place a little better. He was an incredible skier, fast and strong and clean, so fit that he never seemed to tire. He'd easily ski the whole mountain today. The season was due to end soon, and all the resorts up that way would get very quiet for a while.

Mary Jane and Lee were both busy with some early season guests at Spruce Bay who'd wanted two of the new picnic lunch hampers the resort was offering, with Daisy-designed menus, and who had then checked out, leaving a huge and still sopping red wine stain on the new carpet in their cabin's living area.

"Don't worry," Mary Jane said with a sigh, after Lee reported it. "I've got this. Seen it before." She seemed to be over whatever was bugging her the other day at lunch, when she'd gone all patient and wooden, with no explanation, before very firmly changing the subject.

"We don't leave it to Angela and Piri?" Lee asked. These were their contract cleaners, who came in as needed.

"No, because if it won't come clean enough, I want to take the responsibility for it. If it's really bad, we might have to get the carpet store guys back to shift the carpet around or patch it. What is it about brand-new carpet that attracts red wine? It's like it's magnetic!" She set off for the cabin in question, armed with two buckets of different cleaning supplies, and marching with intent.

And just a few minutes later, the honeymooners rolled in, glowing with sun-kissed color and happiness. They'd been out of touch all week, with just the occasional honeymoonish photo or silly text, Whee! Jet boating! for example—showing up on Mary Jane's phone. They had no idea about any changes in Lee's life.

At Mary Jane's prompting, Lee had called their mom and dad and told them her news, and they were thrilled about the baby. "Our first grandchild!"

But they couldn't quite hide their questions and concerns about the lack of a committed relationship. She'd told them, "We're working on it, Mac and I," so that Mom and Dad would realize it was a joint project, not a battleground.

Even if occasionally it was.

Mom was already talking about coming up for a visit, and planning a longer stay to help around the time of the birth, and again Lee felt as if six months was a life-time away and also no time at all.

Weird.

Odd.

The honeymoon couple's return was a little weird, also, to be honest. At the wedding, there had been enough people and activity to distract from any awkwardness, but now it was only the three of them, two climbing out of a vehicle, one standing on the office porch on a mild, sunny day, all of them smiling at each other.

Lee didn't think that Daisy and Tucker were even aware of it, but she was. When she looked at him, she just thought, *Nope, not right. Nice guy, yes, but not interested.* And yet once she'd come so close to marrying the man, and it really spooked her, to be confronted once again with her bad decision.

What was I thinking? How could I have gotten it so wrong?

She couldn't remember all the steps down that mistaken path. She'd taken herself far away from here, not long afterward, largely because she'd wanted to heal herself and rebuild herself in private.

The broken engagement—almost a jilting at the altar, really—had seemed like a massive signal that she didn't really know who she was, and something had told her very clearly that she wouldn't be able to find that out if she stayed here, with Mom and Dad and Mary Jane all tiptoeing around her, biting their tongues.

Lee had made a good life for herself in Colorado for more than ten years, first in Arapahoe Basin, then Aspen. Now she was back, and probably to stay, and she so much didn't want this to be a backward step. She liked who she was now. Self-sufficient. Active. Happy. Independent.

Other people seemed to like her, too.

Mac liked her.

She liked Mac liking her, and she liked him.

But what if being *this* Lee needed conditions that couldn't be met back here at Spruce Bay? What if her return muddied the waters of her decision making, and brought another huge mistake? She kept a guard around herself that she didn't want to let down. She didn't want to change, and definitely didn't want to go back, and—

Well, she didn't really understand it, but seeing Tucker and Daisy just spooked her.

Daisy gave her a warm, giant hug. "So good to see you properly. We barely talked at the wedding. When are you heading back to Colorado?"

"I'm not. Did you come here direct from the airport? Your bags are still in the back."

"Just wanted to say hi on our way through, and make sure Mary Jane didn't need any help after the weekend."

"We didn't have the restaurant open or anything," Lee reassured her. "Only two cabins booked. They loved your picnic hampers, by the way. It's still very quiet here, so we were fine."

"I thought you might have started back already. Wait a minute, you're not, you said? What do you mean, you're not?"

"Stuff to talk about." She waved it all away. "Not now."

"Yes, now," Daisy insisted. "Where's Mary Jane?"

"Defeating a wine stain in cabin 9. Battle to the death, I think. Go home and unpack your bikinis."

"You're pushing me away."

She was.

And Daisy wasn't taking it.

"We said to each other we might stop for coffee, and now we definitely are!" She headed inside, and Tucker followed her at a relaxed amble, grinning in appreciation at the sight of his new wife in take-charge mode. The blondest member of the family, Daisy did things like that so prettily, and with such sparkling energy.

Upstairs in the kitchen, she looked around for a moment and said, "Wow, you really have moved back! You've brought your mugs."

"Which one do you want for your coffee?" Lee drawled.

Her sister laughed. "Don't attempt to distract me with irrelevant details."

"Then you're getting unicorns in the moonlight. So cute you'll puke."

"Don't joke about that, please!" Daisy rested a hand on her lower belly, with an expression on her face that was half grimace, half grin. She added, all coy and feminine, "We have an announcement."

Lee did a double take, while Tucker growled, "So much for not saying anything for a bit, sweetheart."

"You were the one who said we should tell people right away," Daisy answered.

"And you were the one who said we shouldn't, and now you are. After about five seconds."

"Daisy, wait a minute," Lee interjected. "You're saying what I think you're saying?"

She shrugged and grinned even wider. "We jumped the gun on the wedding. Fun honeymoon experience, shopping for a pregnancy test in Nassau." Then she saw Lee's face and stopped grinning. "What's the problem?"

Lee sat heavily in a kitchen chair. "I think this is going to kill Mary Jane."

Daisy sat, too. They'd both forgotten all about coffee. "She's a better person than that, isn't she? I know she wants a man and a family. But she's been so generous about the wedding. She'll be even more generous about a baby, I'm sure. She knew we were planning on trying right away."

Lee took a deep breath. "Not when it's two of us." She closed her eyes. "This is not the way I planned for this conversation to go, by the way."

"Lee! *Lee?*"

"I know." She opened her eyes again. "You haven't even met Mac yet."

Daisy repeated Lee's words from half a minute ago. "Now *you're* saying what I think you're saying? Pregnant, too!"

"Yep."

"Who is—? Well, it's obvious who Mac is. But beyond that, who *is* he? *Where* is he? How long have you known him? Is it serious? Do you have plans? What are you going to—?"

Lee cut in. "Mary Jane pretty much did this, too, even though Mac was standing in the room at the time. If you would pause for breath, I could tell you." She added drily, "And congratulate you."

Daisy laughed. "Well, thanks! Same back at you, sis!" They grinned a little sheepishly at each other.

"Do you have a due date?"

Daisy nodded. "We worked it out. Mid-November."

"Then I'm ahead of you," Lee drawled. "Late September."

"Oh, wow!"

"That is mostly what Mary Jane said. She did really well with it, and then half an hour later she got all prickly when she found out Mac and I haven't even decided to live together, let alone get married. I think she'd just run out of energy for being generous."

"So you've told her. She already knows." Daisy grew thoughtful. "So I'm the one who has to decide whether to hold off a little, so as not to hit her with the double whammy."

"Exactly."

"Hold off?" Tucker said. He looked doubtful.

"It's a tough one," Lee agreed.

"It is," Daisy said. "That's why you're moving back, though? Because of the baby? To be around family?"

"Seemed like a good idea."

"And Mac?"

"Mac moved, too."

"Is there a wedding happening? No, you said you have no plans, and you're not even living together."

"Nope," she said, very firmly, because she was getting a little tired of everyone mentioning marriage and weddings.

Tucker hadn't said anything beyond that one question about holding off, but now he shifted on his feet. "You have to tell Mary Jane as soon as you can."

"You think?"

"Can't turn things like this into secrets. If they come out later, they come out worse."

Daisy nodded, and something went back and forth between them. Lee guessed it was something to do with his father's long-ago affair, and the resulting half brother who was much younger than Tucker. He'd never spoken about that stuff with Lee, which was a pretty good signal, in hindsight, that the relationship had never been right. She'd learned about it from Daisy, not Tucker himself.

"Have to pick the right moment, though," Daisy said.

"But if there isn't a right moment, you have to tell her anyhow," Tucker insisted. "You can't use waiting for the right moment as an excuse."

"Before we tell Mom and Dad? Lee, have you told them about you?"

"Yes, I called a couple of days ago. Sorry, would have let you tell it first, if I'd known."

"No problem. Can't always be neat about these things."

"Exactly, Daisy," Tucker said. "Don't make it so Mary Jane thinks she's the last person to know, because then she'll think you thought she couldn't handle it."

They heard the sound of the door downstairs, then footsteps, and Mary Jane herself arrived. Somewhere along the route from cabin 9, she'd rid herself of the cleaning equipment, but the weariness of battle was written all over her face. "I think it's come out enough," she announced. "You can still see it in a bright light. When it's dry, I'll move a chair to camouflage it a little. Hi, you two, by the way. Welcome back. Is that coffee going?"

It wasn't, because they'd gotten too distracted, but Mary Jane clearly needed some. She turned to Lee's magnificent machine and began the process.

"Not the right moment now," Daisy mouthed to Lee.

She nodded in agreement.

They could wait a little, even if Tucker didn't approve.

Chapter Thirteen

"I see no reason whatsoever why pregnant women shouldn't paint boats," Lee said to the world in general, down by the lake at midmorning on Wednesday.

Maybe not really to the world in general, maybe to Mac, even though he wasn't here.

"It's a little late to get defensive about it, since we are already painting them," Daisy suggested.

"Not quite. We're sanding, not painting."

"I hate sanding. I especially hate these masks." Daisy put hers on again, and resumed the sanding they'd both taken a break from, in order to grab a drink of water. Lee hated the mask, too, but she wasn't letting herself take it off for a second while the sanders were on, because breathing in old paint particles definitely seemed like it would be a bad idea for a pregnant woman.

For early April, the weather was gorgeous, and the fleet of Spruce Bay dinghies and canoes needed a fresh coat of marine paint to match the remodeling of the resort that already made the place look the best it ever had. Gorgeous new deck opening from the restaurant, landscaped barbecue area and pool surround, new garden beds and walkways everywhere, new bathrooms and decor and paintwork. Once the trees leafed out and the new spring plantings took hold and began to flower, it would be truly beautiful here.

The electric sanders shattered the lakeside peace with their noise, but another half hour of it brought the hulls of two boats to a smooth finish, ready for a final wipe with thinner before they began to paint. There were eight boats altogether, and they planned to spread the work out, tackling them two at a time. Since their father had given his best attention to the boats and had sanded and repainted them almost every year, they needed only a light refresher coat.

"Painting is much more peaceful than sanding," Daisy said. She opened the can and began to stir. Dad had always gone for a bright sky-blue, a color that, no matter where she encountered it now, always reminded Lee of summers on the lake, and cold, peaty-fresh water, and that unique, musical sound of water slapping on a boat hull. "Mmm, not loving these fumes!" Daisy added.

"I wouldn't do this if we were in an enclosed space," Lee agreed. "But I'm not putting that mask on for this part! Turn away from the paint can when you breathe."

"Yeah, that's better. And you're right, it's fine as soon as I'm away from the can. The breeze takes the fumes away."

"You haven't said anything to Mary Jane yet, have you?" Lee asked, after they'd been painting for a few minutes.

It seemed so strange that they were both pregnant at the same time, yet in such different circumstances. Some sisters in Daisy's position would have been a little miffed at Lee for getting in first. Baby announcements belonged to radiant new brides, not independent single women with no marriage plans and a new boyfriend whom the rest of the family had barely met.

"Still trying to pick my moment," Daisy said.

"You were out shopping for poolside furniture with her for three hours yesterday. There wasn't a moment during that?"

"I didn't want to spoil it. We had fun with it, stopped for coffee and cake halfway through, had some really good laughs."

"I love the look of what you ordered."

"Delivery in three weeks, good to have it in place, although probably a little soon for guests to want to sit out there," Daisy said.

"Except on a day like this. You have to tell her, Daisy. I think Tucker is right about that. And Mac thinks so, too."

"That's because Mary Jane isn't their sister."

"I think that helps them to see more clearly. If she knew we were out here right now, for example, talking about how to protect her feelings…she'd hate that."

"She would. But I don't know what to do about it."

"Bite the bullet. Then ride it out. Only way."

"You tell her, then."

"You know that would be worse. It's not my news to tell."

Daisy sighed. "I know."

Mary Jane appeared an hour later, when they were almost done. "I thought you two could do with some lunch. It's just sandwiches. Shall I bring them out here or do you want to come in?"

"Bring them out," Lee said. "It's so nice today."

"If you're working hard physically, or wearing a jacket!" Mary Jane had been indoors all morning, working on the summer reservations that were starting to come in.

"So put on a jacket! By the time you get back, we'll

have the brushes soaking and our hands clean, and we can have a picnic."

"It would be fun, the three of us," Mary Jane agreed. "How long has it been since we've sat and had a picnic on the dock? Since we were kids, almost. You guys never came back here in the summer, or at least not both at the same time."

"She's handing it to us on a plate," Daisy said after Mary Jane had gone back.

"And you're not talking about a sandwich."

"Nope."

"Just say it."

So Daisy did, when the three of them were sitting in a row, chicken salad sandwiches in hand, with their legs dangling off the edge of the dock, and their butts warmed by the wooden planking that had heated in the sun. "Guess what, Mary Jane? Tucker and I have some news."

"Oh, you do?"

"We're having a baby in the fall!"

Mary Jane's sandwich stopped halfway to her mouth. "What, you, too?"

"Yes, about two months after Lee."

"You'd already told Lee, obviously."

"Well, it just came up. You know how it is."

"This morning," Mary Jane said. "I guess it would, with the two of you out here." Lee opened her mouth to say no, actually, not that morning, but Sunday afternoon, pretty much as soon as they saw each other. But before she could get the words out, however, Mary Jane went on speaking. "That's so great! That is really great news! I am so happy for you!"

She sounded it, too. She really did. No need to tell her that she'd been the last to know.

"This is wonderful! This is fabulous!"

And yet Lee could tell it wasn't completely sincere. Beside her, she could almost feel Daisy picking up on the difference, too. Mary Jane was saying all the right things. Doing the right things, also. Trying like anything to be generous enough not to mind...for the second time this week.

Mary Jane hugged Daisy, who was the one sitting in the middle. She asked for details on due date, and how Tucker felt, and whether they were hoping for a girl or a boy. She said yet again how happy she was. "Two babies together! That is so cool!"

Really impressive performance, sis.

Lee's heart went out to her, and if she hadn't been so sure that moving positions on the dock so that she could hug her and tell her she totally understood how hard this was for her would...well, would have been the worst thing in the world, she would have been there in a heartbeat. Mary Jane didn't want her cover blown.

Daisy did the same as Lee—pretended she didn't know how much Mary Jane was pretending.

Because sometimes that was what you did when you loved someone.

You let them think they had you fooled.

"So we both pretended we couldn't see that she was upset underneath," Lee told Mac that evening, in his cabin.

He'd been running errands all day, dealing with practicalities about the new job and the house rental, and they'd met here, as agreed, at five. Inwardly, he was still a little...upset...himself, to discover that she and Daisy had been sanding and painting half the day, and the fact that Lee had taken a nap after lunch wasn't quite good enough.

Tomorrow, if the weather was still holding, he planned to "help"—translation: take over—and he honestly didn't know if that would annoy her, or if he was right to think it would be better if she wasn't doing this. But he had nothing else on, and he hated this hiatus before the new job started, so why not paint boats? It would stop him from having to coach and deliver pep talks to himself about it.

She's only three months pregnant. She's out in the open, where the fumes can spread. She had a mask on when she was sanding. She took breaks and drank water. It's just painting, not shooting ten meters into the air on a board above an icy curve of snow.

"So how did you know she was upset?" he asked now, about Mary Jane.

"Sometimes you just know."

"Why didn't you call her on it? Tell her you understood that it was a little hard for her?"

"Because we didn't need that, any of us."

"I guess not."

"Sometimes, pretending isn't a bad thing," Lee said.

Like I'm pretending I'm not upset about you painting boats.

Things came in threes, sometimes. His phone rang about a minute later, before they'd had time to decide if they were going out to eat or getting something in, or if they weren't even thinking about food yet, because the bed looked so inviting through the open bedroom door.

"Mac?" It was his mother, in Idaho.

"Hi, Mom. How's it going?"

"Well, not great," she said. "A little sad, actually,

even though we didn't know him that well. Ronnie Halpern died."

"Oh. I'm sorry to hear that." Mac added after a respectful moment, "Who is Ronnie Halpern?" He telegraphed to Lee that this might take a while, but in fact it didn't.

Ronnie Halpern, widower aged eighty-nine and an old friend of Dad's father, had passed away peacefully in a rest home in Pittsburgh, Pennsylvania, surrounded by his loving family, and Mom and Dad were flying east for the funeral on Friday.

"And then we thought we'd come up and spend a day or two with you," Mom said, inappropriately bright, considering. "Friday evening through Sunday afternoon. We've checked flights. There's a red-eye we can take to Pittsburgh tomorrow night, but we just wanted to make sure it would be okay with you before we make the reservation."

"It's fine. It'll be good to see you." Even though he'd seen them only a couple weeks ago. "Email me your flight details and I can pick you up at the airport. You'll fly into Albany?"

"That's right. It would be great if you could pick us up."

But he wasn't quite getting this. Flying all that way for the funeral of someone they'd barely known?

Then he remembered the date.

Saturday was the seventh anniversary of baby Kelly's death.

Sometimes, pretending wasn't a bad thing....

He felt his throat tighten, and knew if he tried to call them on it, tell them they didn't have to do this, that he didn't *want* them to do it, he'd probably not be able to speak at all. Did they know that he'd guessed? That he'd been thinking on and off about that early April date that came every year?

Most of those years he'd gotten a card or an email from Sloane saying things he didn't want to hear. On the second and fifth anniversaries, he'd gotten a phone call from her and that had been even worse.

But this time the anniversary was different, and Mom and Dad knew it. This time, he was a father-to-be again, and in the same ambiguous situation of being involved with the mother, but with no decision about long-term commitment and plans.

He almost said something.

You owe one to Ronnie Halpern, don't you, for giving you a good excuse to come east?

Nope. Don't. The humor was too black, and the truth too close to the bone. In memory of Ronnie and Kelly, he kept his mouth shut.

"You there, Mac?" Mom said.

"Yep, I'm here. Just thinking about where I'm going to put you."

"Where you're going to put us? Oh, wait, Dad wants to speak to you about that."

There was a slight flurry of noise, then Mac heard his father on the line, saying very firmly, "Put us in a good hotel."

"Really?" It wasn't their usual style. Mom was way insistent on economical motel rooms or housekeeping cottages.

In the background, sure enough, he heard her saying, "You don't have to do that."

"Ignore her, Mac," Dad said. Then, with his mouth away from the phone, said, "Let me spoil you for once, Gina," and Mac wondered if this, too, was about the anniversary and the funeral. Dad was extra aware, right now, of the things he held dear, and Mom was at the top of that list.

She came back on the line. "It's fine," she assured him. "Whatever you want is fine."

"No, I'll do the hotel, the way Dad wants. You deserve a little spoiling."

"Well, that would be wonderful." She knew. They both knew. And like Lee and her sisters this morning, neither of them was going to say it out loud.

When he'd put down the phone, he told Lee that his parents were detouring up here to see him after coming east for a funeral, and endured her condolences and good wishes without admitting to the truth of what he knew. It wasn't old Mr. Halpern's death that was weighing on his parents' hearts nearly so much as little Kelly's.

"So...eat in tonight, or go out?" Lee asked him, when there wasn't anything more to say about his parents' plans.

"Out." Should he have told her why they were really coming? He couldn't remember how precise he'd been when he'd first talked to her about his loss. He'd said it would soon be seven years since Kelly had died, but he hadn't mentioned the exact date.

"Now?" she asked.

"Getting hungry," he lied. Really, he needed air and space more than food. Should he tell her? What would that do to her first meeting with his parents? It wouldn't likely make anything easier.

They're coming because you're pregnant and it's the anniversary of the loss of their grandchild, and they don't know if I'll find that tough. They're finding it tough, themselves. They're uncomfortable about not being able to put a label on our relationship. They're remembering what it was like, seven years ago, when Sloane was so big on freedom, and they want to know if they can trust you.

He didn't know if he would find it tough, either, and at some level trust was probably still an issue, too.

"Somewhere nice, hey?" he suggested.

"Adirondack Steakhouse? Not that many nice places open all year round up here."

"Sounds good. Steak is always good. I'm going to help you paint tomorrow, by the way."

"Oh, yeah? How come?"

"Because I have nothing else on, and because I won't be able to help the next couple of days after that, with my parents here."

"You don't have to help at all."

"Give a man a break. You know I hate sitting around."

"Wouldn't be because you hate thinking about me painting when I'm pregnant, would it?"

"That, too," he said easily, with a smile. Faking it. Because sometimes pretending was the best you could do.

"So glad you wanted to go out," Lee said, halfway through their meal. "I didn't know how much I wanted steak till the waiter put it down in front of me!"

"Maybe you need iron tablets."

"I don't, because iron is already featured strongly in my prenatal multivitamin. Tonight I'm just *starving!*"

"Let's not have a repeat of the pizza experience."

"I've been feeling tons better the past couple of days. Zesty!"

"That's great." He smiled, but there was something behind it that reminded her of Mary Jane today—a really solid, convincing performance, but a performance nonetheless.

"It *is* the boat painting, isn't it?" she said. "You don't want me doing things like that."

He said nothing for a moment, then admitted, "Okay, yes, but I recognize that's not rational or reasonable, and I'm trying to fight it. I know the cotton-ball treatment isn't necessary."

She reached across the table and put her hand over his. "Thank you. Thank you so much for trying to find a balance." They went back to eating steak, which was tough on conversational flow and gave her time to think instead.

Points for trying. Mac had definitely earned those. How much longer would it be before he didn't have to try, before he just let go and trusted her and *life?* What would happen if he never learned to do that? What would happen if he kept leaning on her, if he forgot all about their relationship because he was so focused on the baby, if their feelings for each other got confused and lost because they'd never had a real chance to work out what those feelings were?

She felt the same mix of care and claustrophobia that her family used to give her, that Tucker had given her during their engagement, after she'd gotten burned.

Just leave me alone, guys, so that I can stay me.

Being *her* had become incredibly important over the years, and yet Lee knew that in some ways she—the person she was—would change with a baby. Would have to. Would be bound to. People did change with parenthood. She wouldn't be the same person anymore. But she wanted to feel her own way forward with that, she didn't want Mac or her sisters or anyone dictating how it happened and where it went.

And it was the same with "us"—if there even was one. She didn't want shared parenthood to be the only thing that defined them, the whole foundation for her and Mac's relationship.

"Maybe we could go out in one of the boats, when they're done," she suggested, grabbing for some time together that had no purpose beyond just that—being together.

"Yeah?"

"I'll even let you do most of the paddling. It's such a great lake to explore—so many little bays and points and islands, and some of them have camps on them, or houses. You can see things you'd never see from the road or the shore. If it's still nice tomorrow, we could paint in the morning and paddle in the afternoon."

"Paddle or row?" He seemed to be holding back a little. "There are dinghies, too, aren't there?"

"I like paddling better, even though you tend to get wetter. And Daisy and I painted two of the canoes yesterday."

"Life jackets?"

"They're in the boat shed. We'll brush the spiders off, I promise, and hang the jackets up all morning in the sun, in case they're musty."

"Food and water?"

"We have waterproof bags for that stuff."

"First-aid kit?"

"You expect me to tell you we don't have one, but we do, and it can go in the bag."

"Cell phones?"

"Great reception now, most of the lake. Way better than it was a few years ago."

"GPS tracker? Flare gun?"

"We... Well, I guess we could—" Okay, no. She sat

back and looked at him. "Who are you kidding here, Mac?"

"Myself. Yeah, just me." He looked embarrassed and wry. "Kidding myself. Not really suggesting a GPS or a flare gun."

"Good answer. You're not that worried about a canoe trip, are you?"

He said reluctantly, "Something could happen."

"Something could, even if there wasn't a pregnant person on board. We'll tell Daisy or Mary Jane what we're doing. We won't go miles from shore or across to the far side. And apparently you'll be doing most of the paddling, so the pregnant person won't even get tired." She leaned across the table and planted a slow and very smoky kiss on his mouth. He tasted salty. "I like that we're talking about this," she told him softly. "Solving it. Meeting each other halfway."

He muttered, "Yeah…" and kissed her back with his heart not quite in it, she could tell. He was trying. They both were. What if trying never got them very far?

Let it go for now, Lee.

Maybe they'd talked about it enough. She decided to tell him instead what she planned to do to him when they got back to his cabin, and he seemed to find that topic of conversation far more entertaining.

The fine weather held, and Daisy, Mac and Lee sanded and painted four more boats in the morning. Then Daisy went off to do some menu planning for the restaurant, and Mac and Lee put on life jackets, packed a picnic and emergency supplies, and went out on the lake in a sky-blue canoe.

Today, it all seemed so simple, Mac thought. Lee sat in front of him, giving suggestions about where they went, while he worked the paddle, a little clumsily at first because he hadn't done this for a while, then with increasing confidence and rhythm.

They both wore shorts and running shoes topped with sweaters, windproof jackets and the chunky life vests, and she had a New York Giants winter hat, as well, in red, navy and white, with a big colorful pompom on top. She looked ridiculous and he kept grinning at her, and it was lucky he was behind her and she couldn't see the grin, or he would have had to explain.

The contrast between Lee in tiger mode last night in bed, sliding her naked body against his, and Lee in outdoor mode today, making the canoe rock from side to side when she twisted to point out the landmarks from her childhood, tickled him down to his toes.

He loved that she was like this.

All woman, deceptively packaged.

He loved that a lot of men wouldn't have looked twice at her, because they were blind to what really counted, and he knew so much better than them. He felt like the star member of a club of one, because he knew how great she was and how gorgeous she was and how fun she was, beneath the knit football hat and concealing jacket and vest.

When they beached the canoe on a tiny, uninhabited island and she climbed out of it, he loved the smooth, silky stretch of her bare legs, the curve of her butt in the denim shorts and the nice knots of muscle in her calves. He loved the way she scrambled up the path, and the way she paused for a moment and closed her eyes to breathe in the air, full of the scents of earth and pine and early spring.

He loved the eagerness in her face when she said, "There are some rocks over the other side, beyond the pine trees. They should be in the sun, and our legs'll stay warm and we can eat, and we'll have great views all up and down the lake."

They'd had tuna melts for lunch back at the resort, so this was just a snack—doughnuts and bananas and juice. She was a little overoptimistic about how warm it was, even on the sunny rocks, and after a few minutes he saw the goose bumps appear on her legs. "Hey, you're cold...." he said, and shifted the remains of their doughnut picnic out of the way so he could put his arms around her.

She shrugged and gave him an upside-down smile. "Nah, it's okay. Top half is warm. How about you?" She twisted to look at him, her mouth an inch away and so pink and lush from this angle. With the pregnancy, with his baby inside her, she was glowing, ripening, beautiful.

"I have body hair to protect me. You're so smooth...." He leaned into her side and ran his hand along the top of her thigh, where her skin felt like bread dough kneaded to a sheen, or like buttery-soft leather in a high-end car. Were those the kinds of images you were supposed to have when you touched your lover's skin? He didn't care. This was who she was to him—a woman of depth and quality, utterly real.

I love her. I just love all of her.

It kicked the bottom out of his world, it was so scary, and he didn't know what he was going to do about it. His heart began to thump faster, and he almost said it then and there. But it was only just over a week since they'd had that whole conversation about not getting married, and it hadn't gone well.

She'd been angry about the very idea. She'd thought he was assuming that she was hanging out for a proposal, and she'd bristled at the idea of being taken for that kind of traditional female. He did understand that.

Did *I love you* fall into the same category?

He wasn't sure.

I love you was about now, not about the future, so it should be a little safer. But he knew that it could sound like a statement of ownership or a piece of emotional blackmail, just as much as *I want to marry you*.

If she thought this was just about the baby…

If it *was* just about the baby…

Was that why he was feeling like this? Did he feel this surge of love only because she was the woman carrying his child?

Maybe the *L* word and the *M* word were both best avoided.

Lee had just picked up his hand and put it back on her thigh. The inside of her thigh. Mac wanted to laugh at the idea that he was thinking about love and marriage while she was clearly thinking about sex. How was that for a role reversal? But if he laughed, she would demand to be let in on the joke, and then it would stop being funny.

They'd known each other less than four months. His sister, Lisa, had dated Andy for three years before they got engaged and another year before they got married. His parents only a little less than that.

For him and Sloane, it had been nearly eighteen months from when they met to when they parted in such grief and turmoil. And if they'd said, "I love you, let's get married," at any point during that time, he thought it would have only made the situation even worse.

Seven years on Saturday since it had all happened, and if the anniversary, and his parents' unacknowledged gesture in coming here for it, were a part of what he was feeling right now, he didn't know how to separate out the strands.

Should I tell Lee about the anniversary?

Bottom line, he still didn't trust himself on this. Didn't trust his head or his gut. He didn't know what he should be looking for, or what she really wanted for the future—not six months from now when the baby came, not a year from now, not ten.

Although apparently she knew what she was looking for right this minute—a little action, a little taste and tease for what might happen later. The bed in his cabin had a big dip in the middle, and it rolled them into each other's arms all night long. He was getting pretty attached to that.

Maybe he should just think about sex, too. Any other subject had too many ramifications. The ramifications of sex, on the other hand, they'd already gotten into trouble with, so in a weird way they were safe. One of the unsung benefits of pregnancy—you didn't have to think about contraception anymore.

"You're right, you're not cold," he told Lee, as she pressed her thighs together, imprisoning his moving hand. "Along up here…in here…you're warm as anything." He touched her, and turned his cheek against hers, then turned it a little farther so that their mouths met in a long, unhurried kiss.

Chapter Fourteen

Mac's parents flew into Albany at six-thirty on Friday evening, and he drove down to pick them up. He'd made a reservation at the Adirondack Steakhouse for the four of them at seven-thirty, even though he and Lee had already eaten there once this week. She was still craving red meat, and he'd teased her about it this morning, when she'd confessed that she wanted a repeat visit.

"That's my woman. None of this nonsense about chocolate, or ice cream with pickles on top. We got man-size cravings here."

"Predicting a boy?"

"Nope, just proud of you."

"Proud because I'm craving red meat?"

"Proud of you because I'm just proud of you."

And in an hour, he would be introducing her to his parents. He was swinging past the hotel he'd booked for them, so that they could check in and unload their bags, and then they were meeting her at the restaurant.

Lee prepared for the evening with a nervous need to make a good first impression.

How did you do that, when you were already pregnant? And especially when you had no marriage plans? Those could be a protective shield at a time like this, and she was shocked at herself for wanting the shield, when it was just another item on her rapidly growing list of bad reasons to get married.

Meanwhile, she wasn't a dress kind of girl, and the waistbands on most of her pants were beginning to feel a little tight. She ended up choosing some black stretch jeans with the top button unfastened, and a draped white top that came low enough to conceal the fact, then put on heels and makeup and jewelry so that the outfit wouldn't look too casual.

Because she didn't want to be late—the whole good-first-impression thing *remember?*—she arrived ten minutes early, while it took longer than Mac had expected for his parents to check in to their hotel, so they didn't arrive until nearly a quarter to. This meant almost twenty-five minutes of sitting at the restaurant's bar on her own, checking the periodic texts telling her, We're just about to leave, and Sorry, my mom is changing her purse.

When she turned for the fifth time at the sound of the restaurant's front door opening and it was them at last, the relief must have shown all too clearly on her face—and maybe the anxiety, too. She scrambled down from the bar stool, wondering when she'd last been this nervous and self-aware.

"Hi…"

"We made it." He added for her ears alone, "Betcha you were wondering if we ever would."

"Little bit."

He pulled her against him to drape his arm around her shoulder, linking them together, and said to his mom and dad, "Well, this is Lee, obviously." And he forgot to let her go, so that his mother, who'd been coming in for a greeting hug, had to stop on a dime and turn it into a handshake instead.

His father stood back a little. "Lee. It's good to meet you." He stuck his hand out also, and she had to lean forward and out of Mac's cloaking arm in order to reach. Mr. Wheeler was gray-haired and blue-eyed, but had the same strong, hard build as his son, and almost the same voice.

Lee could immediately see where Mac had got his athleticism from, while from his mother he'd inherited his coloring. She had inky-black eyes, olive skin that was still beautifully smooth and thick black hair with only threads of gray.

Lee had a baby inside her carrying this same genetic heritage of dark coloring and athletic build, and she couldn't help wondering how it would mix with the legacy from her side. What hair color did you get if you mixed caramel and dark chocolate? Would the baby's eyes be blue-green or brown?

Once more, she was confronted with how momentous this was, and how much scope there was for everything to go wrong. These two people had already lost a grandchild, one who'd been conceived by accident in an uncertain relationship. Lee could easily see how they might distrust her, or want things from her that she couldn't give. The pressure was huge.

The Wheelers were formally dressed, him in a dark suit, her in a rather somber gray-and-white dress, and Lee remembered that they'd been at a funeral today. Clearly, they hadn't had a chance to change their clothes, and she thought Mac had probably hurried them away from their hotel room too fast because he'd known that she was waiting, and nervous.

"I'm sorry about..." she began, but in the heat of all these new impressions, she couldn't remember the name of the old friend they'd just lost. An elderly man's

name, she thought. Stan or Reg or…"Ron." It came to
her, thank goodness. "Ronnie. Mr. Halpern."

"It was a lovely funeral," Mrs. Wheeler said. Gina.
Her name was Gina, and his dad was Paul, Lee coached
herself inwardly. Did they want her to use their first
names? So far, they weren't saying, and she didn't want
to make assumptions.

Sometimes, people were invited to call their child's
future grandparents Mom and Dad, and she really didn't
want them to ask her for that. Not yet. Maybe not ever.
She would be acutely uncomfortable about calling them
something that implied closeness and intimacy and love,
if those things didn't exist between them.

Mac had said, "This is Lee, obviously," but there was
so much about this that wasn't obvious at all. She felt as
if she was stuck on stage without a script. Her hand in
Paul's grip had felt like a chunk of ham, and she could
hear her own pulse beating in her ears.

"More of a celebration," Gina added, about the funeral. "He'd been ready to go, his daughters said."

"Much easier when someone's had a good span of
life," Paul agreed.

A server showed them to their table, and Lee sat beside Mac and opposite his mother. The appearance of
menus was a relief. They were big, laminated and folded
things that she could hide behind, pretending to be faced
with an impossible amount of choice, and they could
talk about those choices. What did Gina think looked
good? Was she thinking she'd have dessert later on?

An hour and a half later, Lee still hadn't relaxed,
even though outwardly everything had gone fine. Gina
had said, "Call us Gina and Paul," so that was one small
problem out of the way. Mac's mom loved what she'd
seen of the hotel, she said. "Such a beautiful setting,

right on the lake, almost on an island, and it's such a beautiful old building. I hope we can explore the whole place tomorrow, maybe eat in one of the restaurants there tomorrow night."

She seemed warmer than Mac's father, or maybe she had a woman's knack of pretending better, of finding the small talk that distracted from any undercurrents.

There were definitely undercurrents. Mac's parents seemed even more anxious than Lee felt, studying their son's expressions too closely, talking about generalities in an overly bright way that suggested there was something on their minds that they didn't want to mention.

It wasn't Lee's pregnancy. They'd mentioned that. Gina had asked her how she was feeling, and Paul had assured her gruffly that she could trust Mac to take care of her, because he'd been raised the right way.

But when people had been raised the right way and they were having a baby together, they usually got married, or at least made some kind of statement about their long-term commitment. Was Paul hinting that he expected that? Was this the source of the tension? The Wheelers wanted all this to fall into neat, conventional lines, and didn't quite know how to manage without them.

Paul called for the check, then said to his son, "What are we doing tomorrow? Let's make a plan." He looked restless, and eager to have a concrete decision, and a schedule. "There must be some good hiking around here. Or maybe take a boat out on the lake. You know I hate sitting around."

"Paul!" Gina protested. "Is that really how we want to spend our time with Mac and Lee while we're here? Sightseeing?"

"I don't see why not. Hope you're not suggesting

we go shopping or sit in a café for hours. That would drive me crazy."

Gina laughed and punched him gently in the arm. "Paul, I've been married to you way too long to think that shopping and sitting is ever going to be on the agenda. Okay, I guess you're right. We should plan something to do. We could hike tomorrow, if Mac and Lee are interested."

"I'm in, if Lee is," Mac said.

"Lee? Are you?" Paul seemed gruffly eager, and she understood where he was coming from. If this indefinable awkwardness was going to continue, she much preferred to disguise it with something active, also. The restaurant meal had been a strain on all of them, at some level, despite the flow of conversation.

"I always like to be out-of-doors if I can," she told him.

"Any suggestions about a route?"

"We could go out to the point of Tongue Mountain, where the ridgeline meets the lake. That's a nice trail, no steep parts, and great views of the water at the end."

"Sounds beautiful," Gina said. "And not too strenuous."

"Mac," his father said, "could you grab some snacks and water bottles for us, and bring a day pack?"

"Sure."

"So tomorrow we'll have breakfast at the hotel, and then set out," Paul decreed, and it was settled.

"You coming back to my place?" Mac asked Lee quietly on their way out of the restaurant. He stood close, letting his fingers dangle at his side so that they tangled with hers. They clasped them together for a moment and squeezed, and it felt good, a secret connection and confirmation.

"If you want me."

"Of course I want you. Was it okay tonight? What did you think?"

"I like them," she told him truthfully. "I can see parts of you in them."

"Little tense, though, couple of times at the beginning. There's—"

"It was," she agreed. "I can't see how it couldn't be, even though we were all trying so hard."

"You don't have to do that," he told her, but she couldn't see how to avoid it.

"What were you going to say? Before I cut in."

"Nothing. It's fine. Can't talk here, anyhow. They'll be waiting outside."

"So I'll see you after you've dropped them off?" she asked.

"Probably twenty minutes or so, I guess."

"I'll be there, sheets prewarmed." She had a key to his cabin. She liked having a key.

"And I do like my sheets prewarmed." He gave her a quick kiss and then hurried to catch up to his parents.

Chapter Fifteen

As soon as Mac thought he'd be in range, he held out his key fob and pressed the button on it, so that the pickup gave a little whoop and unlocked itself, lights flashing. Mom and Dad were still ahead of him and he didn't want them standing beside the car in the cold while he caught up.

He had almost told Lee about the anniversary just now, but the timing was wrong. And the place—standing in the small entrance of a restaurant, parents waiting for him out here. Lee looking more tired and wrung out than she was admitting to; his dad trying so hard to like and trust her, but deeply suspicious.

Mom was more generous in that area. Dad liked to know where he stood, and right now Mac could tell that he didn't have any idea. If there'd been an engagement announcement, Mom would have been the one gushing and tearful, but Dad would actually have been the happiest.

Marriage was neat. It let you think that you understood what was happening, even when you really didn't. Dad would have been totally placated by a wedding in the works, and he would have been wrong.

Mac climbed into the vehicle, waited until they were both strapped in and then set off. They were quiet at first, until Mom broke the silence. "She seems lovely, Mac. I liked her a lot."

"Good," he answered. "Because I like her a lot, too."

He waited for one of them to ask about their plans, but they didn't, and he knew their silence indicated an inner struggle. He wished he could have satisfied them, but he didn't know how. At the hotel, he made sure they were settled and comfortable, and then headed back to the cabin, his heart giving a lurch when he saw the lights behind the closed drapes, and Lee's shadow moving around inside.

"Hey, you promised me warmed sheets," he told her.

"Sorry." She gave him an upside-down grin. She was wearing a fluffy robe, and nothing but clean skin underneath. He could see that her hair was wet at the ends. "Decided I wanted a shower, and stayed in there too long. You were quick, dropping them off."

"I didn't stay. Didn't even turn off the engine." He folded her into his arms and smelled the shower freshness of her.

"I'm secretly glad about that," she whispered in his ear.

"Oh, secretly?"

"Well, I'll let you in on the secret, but no one else."

"No?"

"See, I really, really wanted to be awake when you got back, but I wasn't sure how long that was going to last."

"Are you proposing fast sex or sleepy sex?"

"Whatever you've got."

"I probably have both."

"Both is good."

"We'd better get down to it, then." He peeled back the robe, kissed her bared shoulders, then let the garment drop to the floor. He stripped, and she was waiting for him in the bed by the time he got there.

He wanted to treat her as if she was made of glass. He kissed her slowly, all the way up her body and then all the way down, cupping her breasts so gently that his hands seemed as if they were made of paper. She whimpered for more and he told her she was wicked.

"You like me wicked," she pointed out.

Truthfully.

"I like you any way you want to be."

That was true, too.

Mostly.

"What if I want to be fierce tonight?" she said.

"You can be fierce."

She laughed and rolled him over so that she was poised on top, and she felt so amazing, all heavy and round and squishy, but he wouldn't let her be as fierce as she wanted because the protectiveness kicked up another notch, and he didn't know how to make it go away.

Something else went away, instead.

"What's up?" she whispered.

Hell, should he tell her?

"Nothing's up," he answered, playing for time. He lay there, breathing hard, while she eased herself off him and lay pressed against his side, head pillowed in the crook of his arm, one leg between his, fingers lazy on his chest and stomach and groin.

"Something is."

Telling her about the anniversary seemed like ruining the party, like spilling a jug of iced water on a perfect hot meal. It seemed like inviting her into a private place, only to shut her out again seconds later. It seemed like inviting someone else into the bed, and he'd never been into the idea of a threesome.

"It's fine," he insisted. "Disappointed in myself."

It was true, and ambiguous, and she got distracted by it, thinking he was talking about the failure of his performance.

Which turned out to be very temporary. Her fingers worked some magic, and then so did the rest of her body, and he forgot everything and just gave himself to the pure high of making love to her, and then the peace of falling asleep with their bodies wrapped together.

In the night, waking to find her arms flung across his stomach, he decided not to tell her about the anniversary until after his parents had gone. Time enough then. It wasn't dishonesty, it was kindness—to her, to his parents and to himself. Maybe even kindness to Sloane. The decision felt like a relief, and Mac let all the dark, sad feelings go for now. He rested his palm on her lower belly and felt the first suggestion of a baby there, the gentle curve of a bulge.

Different.

It was very different to last time.

Much, much better.

"I was serious about the sleepy sex, by the way," she murmured beside him.

"Oh, yeah? How did you know I was awake?"

"When you put your hand on the baby."

"That was enough to wake you up?"

"Don't apologize."

"I'm not."

"I love it when you put your hand on the baby."

"And I'm very happy to have woken you up enough for sleepy sex." He began to touch her in all the ways he knew she loved, and she stretched and made some creaky, lazy sounds. It was perfect, and he told himself not to think about anything else.

* * *

They met Gina and Paul for a buffet breakfast at the hotel at eight-thirty, and spent almost as long over the meal as they'd spent at dinner the night before. Their table by the window gave glorious views down the lake, with shadings of blue mountain reflected in sparkling water. The sun was shining and the promise of spring was strong in the air. The crocuses were blooming in the hotel gardens and the grass had begun to green up again, after losing its winter covering of snow.

Paul was the first to be ready to leave. "I need to get my hiking boots on. Gina, you're not having more coffee, are you? What if we lose this beautiful sun?"

She sighed good-humoredly and said, no, three cups was probably more than enough. When he left the table to go up to their room, she lingered long enough to tell Lee, "He's not always this antsy. You'll be wondering how I put up with him."

"No, Gina, I understand how he feels. I get restless if I'm indoors too long, just as he does."

"Then you and Mac are very well suited," she said, then pressed her fingertips over her mouth as if she thought she'd said the wrong thing.

Which maybe she had.

Lee tried to find a safe response, but couldn't. Mac was shifting on his feet. "You changing into hiking boots, too, Mom?"

"No, these'll be fine." She showed her foot, clad in a white leather athletic shoe. "You said the terrain was fairly easy, Lee?"

"Yes, it's a vehicle track, goes up and down a little in places but is mostly flat, and covered with a carpet of pine needles in lots of places."

"Snakes?"

"Still asleep, till May."

"Good to know."

It was a beautiful walk, and when Lee mentally compared it to the alternatives Paul had disdained—shopping and sitting around—she had to agree with him. As a way of getting to know Mac's parents without pressure, this was so much easier. They were interested in the animal and plant life of the area, so she talked about that, and they told her she was as good as a professional guide. She filed it away as something to think about for later, after the baby was born, because she wasn't sure that working at Spruce Bay would really be the right thing for her in the longer term.

Back at Mac's pickup, they decided they didn't need lunch, since breakfast had been so lavish and they'd snacked on chocolate and nuts during the walk. With his energy undiminished, Paul proposed, "Let's rent a motorboat at the hotel." So they spent three more hours out-of-doors while Lee directed them to several beautiful spots on the lake that you couldn't get to by road.

It was five o'clock by the time they returned the boat. There was a change in the air, promising a spring dump of snow, and the sun had gone from the lake, leaving the wind cold and making Lee realize how tired she was.

Mac could see it, too. He did the thing he'd been doing a lot since his parents got here: standing close to her and letting their fingers twine together down by their thighs, and it made her melt, because it was so intimate and private and tender. "Do you want to skip dinner with us? It's been too much for you today. Mom is right, you've been our tour guide all day and you haven't had a moment."

"I've really enjoyed it," she said truthfully.

"That's not the point."

"No?"

"Take a break. Let me drop you back at the cabin and bring you some takeout, and you can watch TV till you fall asleep. I'll creep into bed beside you later on."

"You just want more sleepy sex."

"You saw right through me," he drawled. "Can you agree to this, though? Please? Or I'm going to worry about you. You really look wiped, and you've been so great with my parents all day."

"I like them." It was getting easier. They were her kind of people. It was the situation that they all struggled with, not each other.

"But you can take a break from them tonight. What can I get you? Chinese food from that place with the deck and ramps, near the theme park?"

"It sounds good," she admitted, because now that she'd acknowledged how tired she was, it seemed to have seeped right into her bones. She was so exhausted that she ached all over, her teeth hurt and she wanted to cry in Mac's arms.

He took her back to the cabin, and she called her sisters to let them know what was happening, because she hadn't seen them since before dinner last night.

Daisy said, "You do sound like you need a nap. I'm getting to know that feeling. See you whenever. There's snow in the forecast for tonight, did you know?"

"Yes, I could feel the change starting after we'd been on the lake."

"Well, wrap up warm in that cabin, because it'll probably be three or four inches deep by morning. Not supposed to last long, thank goodness."

Mac was back in half an hour with General Tso's chicken and fried rice, before he disappeared back to his parents at the hotel. Lee ate carefully, including all the broccoli, wearing the robe he'd pulled from her body last night, sitting up in the bed that smelled like him, fresh and warm. She fell asleep with the TV on and didn't even wake up when he crept in several hours later, turned it off and climbed into bed.

Chapter Sixteen

What woke Lee was Mac's phone.

The melody mingled with her dream at first and made no sense, and by the time she worked out what that sound was, he'd lunged out of bed to fumble for the phone on the bedside table and say a croaky "Hello," once he had it to his ear.

It was two in the morning.

Good phone calls didn't come at that hour.

"Hi. Yeah, it's me…." He listened, seated on the edge of the bed. Lee, still disoriented from sleep, had her back to him, but thought he was probably naked because he usually slept that way.

"Because I was asleep," he went on, "so my voice is husky. You don't sound like you, either." He listened again. "Where are you?" There was a pause. "Do you know what time it is here?" Another pause. "No, because I'm not in that time zone, where, even so, it would be midnight."

It went on, and Lee heard almost every word he said, even though he stood up after a few minutes and went into the bathroom and closed the thin door. "I know," he said on the far side of it. "Do you really think I haven't been thinking about it? What do you want me to tell you, Sloane? Haven't we both said everything that can possibly be said? Haven't we both punished ourselves and each other enough?"

To be honest, Lee could have stopped listening at that point. She could have put her head under a pillow and tried to think about something else.

"No, I don't want to," he was saying. "No, I don't think it would help. Yes, I can tell you've been drinking. That's okay, if that's what you want, if it gets you through. No, don't apologize for calling. I'm sorry I said that thing about the time difference—you couldn't have known. I just think these calls and emails on this date every year... Yes, almost every year. I think you missed the fourth.... It's not like I go out of my way to make a note of it, but yeah, I notice.... No, I'm not telling you to *move on.* I'm just—"

This date every year.

That was when Lee finally stopped listening, and only because the thoughts in her head were speaking louder.

This date.

It was Sloane on the other end of the phone, and she was calling because this was the anniversary of the day their baby had died, and yet Mac hadn't told Lee. It was the reason for the extra undercurrent of complicated feeling she'd detected in his parents this weekend and hadn't understood.

No, more than that. It was the reason his folks had come here in the first place. The funeral of an old man they didn't know very well had given them the excuse they needed to check up on their son's well-being and to examine the future mother of the child waiting to be born, so they could make sure she'd keep the coming baby safe, the way Sloane hadn't.

And Mac hadn't told her.

Lee knew why he hadn't. Exactly why.

He was protecting her. He understood the powerful extra layer of tension it would have created if she'd known, and he was protecting her from it. She loved him for it, and it scared her and made her angry at the same time. Plus her head was in such a whirl with all those strong and tangled emotions that it made her dizzy and sick.

It was two o'clock in the morning.

Twelve minutes past, actually, because Mac and Sloane had been talking for a while.

Lee fought a wave of claustrophobia so powerful that she had to push her face into the pillow to stop herself from moaning out loud. She didn't want to stay here.

In the bed.

In the room.

It didn't feel like a cocoon the way it had earlier, eating here all tucked up in bed, knowing that Mac would soon be back. It felt like a prison. She wanted to be out and away, where she could breathe and think and find a direction for her emotional compass.

Right now, it was pointing six different ways at once. She swiveled into a sitting position, feet on the floor, shoulders bent to cradle her churning stomach, the robe she'd fallen asleep in twisted and not very comfortable, and just ached for Mac, facing such a painful anniversary.

Lee understood why Sloane had needed to call, but it was confronting, too. Mac had a shared and fractured bond with someone, a connection that had faded but would never fully go away. The anger and recrimination tied them together as much as it forced them apart, and one strand of what Lee felt right now was actually jealousy.

But there was more.

Their own baby, hers and Mac's, this precious little being inside her, was already being molded and changed by the death of its half brother seven years ago. Mac would be a different father because of it. Gina and Paul would be different grandparents, with different expectations and fears.

Lee herself would be a different mother, and in Mac's pained voice, still sounding through the bathroom door, she could hear the way tiny Kelly's death changed their relationship. Mac was trying to keep his voice low, but he couldn't manage it, and she heard his tone rising again. "All I ever asked was that you acknowledge…" It dropped once more, and she couldn't hear the words.

He was protecting her by not telling her, and she hated it. Loved him. Hated what he'd done.

Wait. *Loved him?*

She did. It was starkly and painfully clear to her in this moment. She'd never dared say it to herself before, because she'd once said it about Tucker Reid, and she'd been horribly wrong.

This was different. The things she felt for Mac she'd never felt for anyone. The sense of joy and peace when she was in his company; the things she understood about him without even trying. The way a silly conversation going back and forth between them could make her whole day, the way sleeping with him could make her whole night.

She loved him, and right now she was angry with him, and aching for him, and scared of the power her feelings gave him, when sometimes what he wanted to do with that power was to protect her more than she needed it. He was so focused on the baby… Did he even *know* how he felt about the baby's mom?

He'd kept this secret about little Kelly from her, and maybe that wouldn't have mattered so much if his parents hadn't chosen to visit, and if Sloane hadn't called.

Protecting Lee was a way of shutting her out. Protecting her was an act of kindness, but it wasn't an act of respect. And if Mac couldn't respect her for who she was—a strong woman, a woman who listened and understood… If he didn't love her for herself, for each other and what they had together as a couple—then this wasn't going to work.

She needed to get out of here. Two in the morning, dressed in a fluffy robe, and all she wanted was to leave so that she could get her balance back.

But she couldn't, because that would push all Mac's buttons, and she loved him too much to do that.

She went to the window and saw that the spring snowstorm Daisy had warned her about was here, with the mix of cold air from the north and moist air from the south making the flakes fall thick and heavy and fast. Lee couldn't possibly do what she wanted, which was to climb into her clothes, grab her keys, get in the car and just drive. It would scare Mac too much.

So she folded the robe more closely around her and went back to bed instead, while the murmuring in the bathroom rose and fell and then finally ended. He didn't come out for a long time. She lay there waiting, listening to the silence in the bathroom, listening for the opening of the door, but nothing happened for minutes on end.

Then, finally, came the sounds and movements she expected. The cautious click of the door opening, the nearly silent pad of his footsteps across the carpet, the careful placing of his phone back on the bedside table, the swish of the covers as he eased himself in beside her.

He thought she was still asleep, so she pretended to

be. Lied to him with her breathing and her stillness, and had him fooled. He didn't fool her. She could hear that he was lying there wide-awake, the breath straining in his tight throat as he lay on his back. She thought he was probably cold because he'd been in that bathroom so long, with nothing but the towel he might have wrapped around his hips. She knew he would be staring through the dark at the ceiling, and she knew what he would be thinking about.

Sloane, the phone call, the baby, the loss. The future... Protecting Lee because she was carrying his child.

Finally, after what seemed like hours and probably was—she had her back to the clock—she couldn't stand the double pretense any longer. She rolled over and held him, discovering that he was warm by this time.

"Sorry. I woke you up," he said.

"Ages ago."

There was a beat of silence as he realized what she was saying. "I thought you were asleep."

"No, just pretending to be. When you got back into bed, I kept trying to sleep, but I couldn't, and I could tell you couldn't, either."

"So you heard, then? It was the phone that woke you?"

The answer to that was obvious, so she didn't bother to say it. "Why didn't you tell me about the anniversary?"

She felt the rise and fall of his chest as he sighed. "Because I— Because with my parents here, it seemed—"

"Don't answer. You don't have to explain. I know why. You were protecting me."

He could tell that wasn't a good thing. "Why is that

wrong? Why is it wrong that I'm trying to take care of you and this baby, and making that my top priority?"

"Because that's not what I want from you."

"What...the hell...*do* you want from me, then?" He said it incredibly gently.

"Nothing. Just this. What we have."

But he didn't understand. "What we have isn't enough for me, Lee." He rolled to face her in the dark. "I love you. I want to marry you. We're having a baby together, and we—"

"Don't."

"Yes. I knew it tonight. It's the right thing to do."

"You said it wasn't, just last week. You made this big argument about it, even when I'd never said it."

"Yeah, and I was wrong. It makes sense of everything, if we get married. When Sloane and I ended that call, I just knew I couldn't...I *can't* keep going the way we are, you and me. Day to day. These vague promises about the future. That we'll do the right thing for the baby. That we won't let anything turn ugly. That we're both on the same team."

"Aren't we?"

"No. We're not. We're separate like this. Transient. We can't ever talk about the future properly because we're so scared of making the wrong assumptions. We're holding back. We're being such cowards. We have to commit to this, 100 percent."

"Would you be saying this if your parents weren't here, and if Sloane hadn't called, and if this wasn't the day the baby died?"

"Maybe not. Not tonight. Probably not. But isn't that the way people come to these realizations? Suddenly? Bolt from the blue? When life hits you in the face and suddenly you know what you want, without question.

I want you to marry me." He squeezed her too tightly, his skin hot against her body, and she felt the force in him. He wanted this so much, and it was wrong.

"No. Mac, the answer is no. I love you, but no." It hurt to say it. It was a horrible word, *no,* when you loved someone and wanted to make him happy, but she had to say it all the same.

"You love me and I love you, and it's still no?" He sounded anguished and frustrated and disbelieving.

"It's not right. We've talked about this. You said it yourself. It's all about the baby."

"Not just about the baby. I love you. I said that. And anyhow, the baby is important."

"The baby is incredibly important, and that's why I won't do it. I won't take the risk that we're doing it only because it's neat and your parents want it and you don't want me to be like Sloane. I love you, Mac, and I won't marry you."

He didn't say anything for what seemed like a long time. "I know you well enough not to try to argue you out of this," he finally murmured.

"Thank you. Because I meant it."

He was silent again, and she could almost feel the desperation in his thinking. "But I can't go on with things the way they are." He sounded broken about it, lost, his voice cracking. "You're in my bed, right now. We made love a few hours ago and it was fabulous, the way it always is. And it makes no sense." He rolled out from under the covers and reached for the pile of clothing he'd left on a chair.

"What are you doing?" She was lost, too.

"Going." He pulled on underwear and jeans.

"Where?" And broken.

"Just for a drive. It's nearly six, getting light." He

dived into the same shirt and sweater he'd been wearing last night. "I'll head over to the hotel and grab an early morning coffee and wait for my parents."

"Want me to come with you?"

"No. No, I don't."

"Why?"

He swore under his breath. "Lee, we have to end this."

"End it?"

"Go back to what we first decided when I came here. That we'll stay connected because of the baby, but not involved. It's the only way I can do it. Ending it. It's the only thing that's going to work."

"Stopping this." She was afraid she wasn't being clear. More afraid about what he was saying. "Stopping *this*." She meant all of it. Did he get that? Bed and laughter and connection. Surely, if he thought about it…

But no.

"It's ended now," he said. "It's over, Lee. Because I can't go on being with you." His voice cracked again. "Being half together and half not. Being together today but maybe not tomorrow. Together in bed, but not on paper. Sharing a baby, but not our lives. And pushing away anything that even smells like a long-term plan because you're so scared we're just doing it for the baby. If we're not making a full commitment to each other and to our future, then we're not together at all, period. I'm sorry." His voice sounded so harsh she thought it must be hurting his throat. "I can't do it any other way."

The flow of words came to an end and he waited, standing there with his whole body practically crackling, wanting her response.

She knew she had to give it to him, and she knew there was only one thing she could say. It was so hard.

Incredibly, impossibly, horribly hard, but she didn't have a choice.

If she crawled off this bed and pushed herself into his arms and started begging and compromising and arguing, if she told him she would marry him just because she didn't want to lose him, she'd be doing the exact thing she was so afraid of—burdening the baby with a marriage that had happened for the wrong reasons.

She took a breath. "Okay."

He said vaguely, as if his speech still left him breathless and without words, "What?"

"I said okay, Mac. I—I can see that's what we have to do."

They looked at each other, pained and shocked and helpless about the point they'd reached so fast and suddenly.

"Yes. It is," he said bleakly.

His feet were still bare. She watched in gut-wrenching silence as he found clean socks and the hiking boots from yesterday, and pulled them on. He didn't look at her while he did it, because that last glance between them had been too unbearable.

Only once he reached the door, with his keys in his hand, did he look back. "I guess I'll see you closer to the time."

For a moment, she didn't understand. "What time?"

"The birth."

And then he left.

It didn't seem real. When she'd left Colorado, she'd driven away from something that had seemed like an interlude, fun and magical but not part of her new life. Having him come after her had given her this illusion that they could go on the same as before, even with a baby in their future. But he was right. They couldn't.

It hadn't worked. He needed all or nothing, and she couldn't give him *all* when the reasons were all wrong, so this was the point they'd reached.

She heard the engine of his truck idling and then picking up speed. There was a blanket of snow on the ground that muffled all sound, and she had to strain to hear that hissing, rumbling noise of him wheeling around to reach the road. The hum of him picking up speed. Now the engine sound was ebbing, and in another few seconds she wouldn't be able to hear it at all.

She felt empty, bereft and lost. Where was the original vision she'd had of herself coming east, reconnecting with her sisters and setting up an independent, satisfying future for herself? Lee couldn't remember how she'd thought that would work, but today—somehow, shockingly—was the day she had to get started on it.

Baby steps, starting with climbing out of bed.

She felt like an old woman, moving stiffly to the bathroom. Mac's bathroom, with his shaving gear sitting beside the sink, and his shampoo on the edge of the tub. She took a shower, feeling as if she had a rock in her stomach as well as a baby. It made her ill. She dressed and made sure she hadn't left anything of hers behind, because she wouldn't be coming here again.

Then she drove through the fall of fresh snow back to Spruce Bay, where Mary Jane and Daisy were about to open the restaurant for home-cooked breakfast, featuring Daisy's signature muffin baskets as well as hot eggs and sides. Lee helped, even though she wasn't really needed.

"You'll need me when we get busier, though," she told her sisters, "So I should get in some practice."

"What's up? You don't look that great," Mary Jane said.

"I'm fine. Didn't sleep well." Because she should

get in some practice at shrugging off questions about Mac, too. There would be a lot of them, no doubt, and at some point she'd have to say, "We've split up." But she couldn't manage to say it yet.

They served a party of ten for breakfast. They were here for some serious fishing, and were done with the meal by eight. Lee, Mary Jane and Daisy cleared up together, and it felt like the first sign that she might actually get through this—alive, if not happy. The restaurant and kitchen were bright and warm, the clouds were clearing away and the sun was coming out, and it was great to talk and laugh as they worked.

"Do we have anyone staying over tonight?" Daisy asked Mary Jane.

"No, all the guests are checking out, then no more bookings till Wednesday. Can't wait till the weather warms up and we're full. I want to see people using the new barbecue area and sitting by the pool, now that it's all so much more inviting."

"Today I'm loving the snow," Daisy said. "So beautiful! Sparkling in the sun."

"It won't last," Lee interjected.

She could hear how downbeat it sounded, but Daisy only teased her. "I know that, ski queen, but there is life after snow, you know."

Life after snow. Life after Mac. Was there?

It was Daisy who enjoyed the snow that morning. Tucker arrived and she went out to meet him, as they'd almost finished in the restaurant, so she wasn't really needed. Resetting the tables by the window, Lee saw them greet each other, and felt a stab of loss so powerful that it froze her in place.

She couldn't look away. Tucker whirled Daisy into his arms and they gazed at each other as if they'd never imagined a moment so precious. He bent to kiss her and she reached to run her fingers through his hair. They grinned at each other, and Lee blinked back tears. The next time she looked they were making a snowman.

It made her think about herself and Mac in Colorado, the way they'd laughed and the way they'd made love, the times they'd been out in the cold fresh air together and the times they'd wrapped themselves up in warmth. All the talking and silliness and shared moments... She ached for it and yearned for it and missed it so much.

She wanted to be with him, and he wasn't here.

It seemed like a loss as extreme and permanent as death, and she wanted him back. She just wanted him back, and she never wanted to have to feel like this again.

"And it's nothing to do with making things right for the baby," she whispered out loud, as the realization came. "It's him. It's just him. I love him. I want him in my life. For the rest of my days. Those aren't the wrong reasons. They're the right ones. Why didn't I know that before?"

"Are you done? Can we close up?" said Mary Jane from the kitchen doorway.

"Oh. Yes." Lee glanced vaguely down at the table. The napkins were missing, but she wasn't going to think about that now.

"You sure you're okay? You've been so quiet and not yourself this morning."

"I think I'm okay."

"But you're not sure."

"I want to marry Mac." She blinked back tears. "I'm certain about that. Not sure about much else, actually." She tried a laugh. It didn't work. "But he asked, and I turned him down, and what if it's too late?"

"He asked and you turned him down," Mary Jane echoed in astonishment.

"Yes. I was scared about our reasons. That's always been important, after Tucker."

"But now you've changed your mind?"

"Yes. Because all this time I've been thinking about the baby, and how we shouldn't do something like that just for our child's sake. But I miss Mac so much, and it's not about the baby at all. It just hit me. I want him so much, and the baby is precious, but it's not a part of the wanting. Not for me, anyhow. But what if it's too late?"

"Let me get this straight. When did he ask you?"

"This morning."

"This morning, about three hours ago, and you're scared it's too late."

Yes, because I'm desperate, and it's been the longest three hours of my life.

"I want to see him. I need to."

"So call. Go. Find him."

"Mary Jane, why are you making it sound as if this is simple?"

"Because I think it is. I think you've made it all complicated in your head because you haven't known each other long, because you have a responsibility to the baby that you would never take lightly, because you made a mistake once before and because you like to be your own person. But Mac *gets* you, Lee, and you get him. I've seen it. You're both in your thirties now, and if you don't know pretty fast by this time whether something clicks or not, then you haven't learned much in life. You and Mac click. You and Mac are *right*. Go fix things, or I'm going to get annoyed."

"Go fix things...."

"Please!"

So she went, scared as a kitten, confused as a rabbit. Where would he be? Still at the hotel with his parents? Could she really just ambush him like that?

But she drove there anyhow. The snow was already melting, dripping from the trees, making the wet vegetation glisten in the sun. The ambush happened in the worst possible way.

Or the best, depending on your point of view.

She met him coming across the huge, grand lobby, carrying his parents' baggage while they walked just ahead of him. He spotted her and put the two suitcases down. His parents saw her and exchanged a look, and she knew he must have told them what had happened this morning, before dawn.

"Can I talk to him?" she almost begged them.

"Of course," Gina said, brief and polite, while her husband gave a stiff nod.

"I'll take all that," Paul said to his son, and he grabbed the suitcase handles, while Mac was still standing there, looking the way Lee had felt a few thousand heartbeats ago when she'd stood by the window in the restaurant, staring out at true love in the snow.

"Outside," Mac said. He went through the glassed-in bar that was opened up to the outdoors in the summer months, but enclosed and warm now. She followed him, and they reached the terrace and went down the steps, where there was a line of crab apple trees beginning to bud beside the stone pathway.

"I've changed my mind," Lee said, and burst into tears.

He held her and she couldn't stop crying enough to speak, which was crazy and frustrating, and eventually he said, very cautiously, "About what?"

"About marrying you."

He didn't answer. Maybe Mary Jane was wrong.

"If you still want to."

He laughed. "Lee?"

"I felt as if you'd died. Like I was never going to see you again, and that I'd be mourning for you and missing you the rest of my life. And all the holding back because maybe you were talking about it for the wrong reasons just seemed so stupid. There's only one reason. You said it, and I couldn't hear it, because I made that mistake before, and I've been so careful ever since about being my own person and making good decisions and knowing the reasons for the things I did. I love you. That's the only reason. I love you. You were right. Can we get married? Will you marry me?"

He was still laughing. "Lucky I'm pretty secure in my masculinity, because now you're the one proposing."

"You did it first."

"Wasn't that well-received, I felt."

"I'm not doing any better a job with it, am I?"

"Nope. You get a few points for the crab apple trees and the melting snow, because they're quite pretty, but that's about it."

"You wanted me to say it with roses?"

"Ah, hell, Lee, I just wanted you to say it." He stepped closer. "And now you are. And that's all that matters."

"Well, this is the point I've been trying to make, yes," she told him with a brazen disregard for truth.

"*All* that matters," he repeated, gathering her close and sending his warm breath through her hair with the words. "I don't care what nonsense you talk."

"I love it when we talk nonsense. That was one of the things."

"The things?"

"That hurt me because I missed them so much. I missed all the things we said to each other, the fun we had, the things we agreed on, the things we did together. And I knew I wanted to marry you for those things, not for anything else. It'll be great for the baby if we're married, but I wanted it for all the other reasons, not for that."

"All the other reasons *and* that," he corrected gently, and once again she knew he was right.

"All the other reasons *and* that," she repeated, and it made such total sense that there was nothing more to say, and nothing to do but kiss him, while the sun shone and the snow melted around them.

Chapter Seventeen

"Tell us as soon as you can when we'll be coming back here for a wedding," Gina told Lee, enfolding her in a warm hug.

"Will it be before or after the baby is born?" Paul asked in turn.

They stood in the departure concourse at Albany Airport, waiting for the boarding announcement. Mac and Lee looked at each other, and he said with a grin, "Give us a break, guys! We've gone from splitting up to getting married in the space of half a day, and still haven't caught our breath. Wedding date comes in a separate announcement."

"I'm so happy about it!" His mom wiped her eyes and gave him a hug this time. "Lee, I don't know if you knew there was another reason we wanted to make this trip...."

"Mac told me," she said.

"I don't think we've been all that fair to you. We were tense. It was a hard time, seven years ago. We questioned a lot of Sloane's choices, and we were afraid we might see some of those same choices being made all over again."

"I know. Mac's been scared about it, too, and that put pressure on both of us. We've worked through most of that, I think."

"That's so good to hear. You look so good together."

"Hope so!"

The boarding announcement came, and Gina and Paul didn't linger, as they still needed to get through security. After they'd disappeared, Mac and Lee were left on their own. "What shall we do?" he said. "Head straight back? Or maybe stop in Saratoga for something to eat?"

"Whatever you want," she told him. "Whatever we feel like. Let's not plan. Let's just drive and see what happens. We're getting married, Mac, and I'm floating on air about it, and as long as I'm with you, that's all that's important." She reached up and touched his face—claiming it, if she was honest.

He didn't seem to mind about that. He put his arm around her and they began to walk through the concourse. "Boy, when you change your mind, you really change your mind!"

"Don't change yours," she said, leaning against his chest and nestling against his beloved body.

"Not planning to. Planning to love you, make a home with you, starting with the rental up north...."

"Buy our own place, when we can?"

"Somewhere close to the snow, and to Spruce Bay. Somewhere with a yard so our kids—"

"Kids?" she interrupted.

"Definitely with an *s* on the end."

"Where they can play," she agreed.

"Yes."

"They can play at Spruce Bay."

"They can."

"They'll love Spruce Bay. I did, my whole childhood."

"Lee, I want to keep this—"

"The floating on air?"

"Feels good, doesn't it?" They'd almost reached the exit, and his pickup was waiting not far away, in the lot.

"Feels wonderful," she agreed.

"Keep it forever? Shall we shoot for that?"

"You know I like to win, and to aim high."

"We're winners already."

"All three of us," Lee said, very firmly, and Mac held her even closer as they walked out into the open air, and into their shared future.

* * * * *

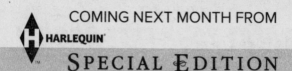

COMING NEXT MONTH FROM

HARLEQUIN

SPECIAL EDITION

Available November 19, 2013

#2299 A COLD CREEK CHRISTMAS SURPRISE
The Cowboys of Cold Creek • by RaeAnne Thayne
When Haven Whitmore is injured on Ridge Bowman's ranch, Ridge steps up—and falls for her. Whether this tantalizing twosome can make it work will depend on whether they can put to rest the Ghosts of Relationships Past.

#2300 HOLIDAY ROYALE
The Bravo Royales • by Christine Rimmer
Innocent Lucy Cordell wants playboy prince Damien Bravo-Calabretti to school her in the ways of romance. What start as lessons in love, however, may well turn into something more.

#2301 THE MAVERICK'S CHRISTMAS BABY
Montana Mavericks: Rust Creek Cowboys
by Victoria Pade
Single and pregnant, Nina Crawford finds herself in trouble when she meets her family's archrival, handsome Dallas Traub. Can Mr. Cowboy and Ms. Crawford find happily-ever-after?

#2302 HER HOLIDAY PRINCE CHARMING
The Hunt for Cinderella • by Christine Flynn
Widowed mom Rory Linfield's new job is a blessing—complete with a sexy, exasperating boss, Erik Sullivan. Rory and Erik are drawn together, thanks to a certain Fairy Godmother and a little Christmas magic.

#2303 AN EARLY CHRISTMAS GIFT
Red Valley Ranchers • by Susan Crosby
Though Jenny Ryder and Win Morgan split years ago, their undeniable chemistry is still there. When Jenny suddenly gets pregnant with Win's baby, they need a little holiday healing to become a real family.

#2304 'TWAS THE WEEK BEFORE CHRISTMAS
by Olivia Miles
Holly Tate is determined to save her family inn, which hunky Max Hamilton wants torn down. Their arguments lead to passion and betrayal, but the Christmas spirit can work wonders....

HSECNM1113

REQUEST YOUR FREE BOOKS!

2 FREE NOVELS PLUS 2 FREE GIFTS!

H HARLEQUIN

SPECIAL EDITION

Life, Love & Family

YES! Please send me 2 FREE Harlequin® Special Edition novels and my 2 FREE gifts (gifts are worth about $10). After receiving them, if I don't wish to receive any more books, I can return the shipping statement marked "cancel." If I don't cancel, I will receive 6 brand-new novels every month and be billed just $4.74 per book in the U.S. or $5.24 per book in Canada. That's a savings of at least 14% off the cover price! It's quite a bargain! Shipping and handling is just 50¢ per book in the U.S. and 75¢ per book in Canada.* I understand that accepting the 2 free books and gifts places me under no obligation to buy anything. I can always return a shipment and cancel at any time. Even if I never buy another book, the two free books and gifts are mine to keep forever.

235/335 HDN F45Y

Name _____ (PLEASE PRINT)

Address _____ Apt. #

City _____ State/Prov. _____ Zip/Postal Code

Signature (if under 18, a parent or guardian must sign)

Mail to the Harlequin® Reader Service:
IN U.S.A.: P.O. Box 1867, Buffalo, NY 14240-1867
IN CANADA: P.O. Box 609, Fort Erie, Ontario L2A 5X3

Want to try two free books from another line?
Call 1-800-873-8635 or visit www.ReaderService.com.

* Terms and prices subject to change without notice. Prices do not include applicable taxes. Sales tax applicable in N.Y. Canadian residents will be charged applicable taxes. Offer not valid in Quebec. This offer is limited to one order per household. Not valid for current subscribers to Harlequin Special Edition books. All orders subject to credit approval. Credit or debit balances in a customer's account(s) may be offset by any other outstanding balance owed by or to the customer. Please allow 4 to 6 weeks for delivery. Offer available while quantities last.

Your Privacy—The Harlequin® Reader Service is committed to protecting your privacy. Our Privacy Policy is available online at www.ReaderService.com or upon request from the Harlequin Reader Service.

We make a portion of our mailing list available to reputable third parties that offer products we believe may interest you. If you prefer that we not exchange your name with third parties, or if you wish to clarify or modify your communication preferences, please visit us at www.ReaderService.com/consumerchoice or write to us at Harlequin Reader Service Preference Service, P.O. Box 9062, Buffalo, NY 14269. Include your complete name and address.

HSE13R

*Damien Bravo-Calabretti was the
Playboy Prince of Montedoro, until innocent Lucy Cordell
asked Dami to be her first. Will this bad-boy prince fall for
the sweet beauty under the mistletoe?*

***

She shook that finger at him again. "Dami, I may be inexperienced, but I saw the look on your face. I felt your arms around me. I felt…everything. I know that you liked kissing me. You liked it and that made you realize that you *could* make love with me, after all. That you could do it and even enjoy it. And that wasn't what you meant to do, when you told me we could have the weekend together. That ruined your plan—the plan I have been totally up on right from the first—your plan to show me a nice time and send me back to America as ignorant of lovemaking as I was when I got here."

"Luce…"

"Just answer the question, please."

"I have absolutely no idea what the question was."

"Did you like kissing me?"

Now he was the one gulping like some green boy. "Didn't *you* already answer that for me?"

"I did, yeah. But I would also like to have you answer it for yourself."

He wanted to get up and walk out of the room. But more than that, he wanted what she kept insisting *she* wanted. He wanted to take off her floppy sweater, her skinny jeans and her pink tennis shoes. He wanted to see her naked body. And take her in his arms. And carry her to his bed and show her all the pleasures she was so hungry to discover.

"Dami. Did you like kissing me?"

"Damn you," he said, low.

And then she said nothing. That shocked the hell out of him. Lucy. Not saying a word. Not waving her hands around. Simply sitting there with her big sweater drooping off one silky shoulder, daring him with her eyes to open his mouth and tell her the truth.

He never could resist a dare. "Yes, Luce. I did. I liked kissing you. I liked it very much."

***

We hope you enjoyed this sneak peek from
USA TODAY *bestselling author Christine Rimmer's new Harlequin Special Edition book,* **HOLIDAY ROYALE,** *the next installment in her popular miniseries The Bravo Royales, on sale December 2013, wherever Harlequin books are sold!*